ABOUT
LAST
NIGHT

ABOUT LAST NIGHT

Laura Henry

bookouture

Published by Bookouture in 2024

An imprint of Storyfire Ltd.
Carmelite House
50 Victoria Embankment
London EC4Y 0DZ

www.bookouture.com

ISBN: 978-1-83525-002-0
eBook ISBN: 978-1-83525-001-3

For Sara

CHAPTER ONE

AUDREY

"Audrey, go. Seriously. I got this."

I look around the apartment I've shared with my girlfriend —ex-girlfriend—and wonder if I'm doing the right thing, sneaking off with half of everything while Shae isn't here. I think of her reaction to a half-empty apartment when she returns. It will be part shock because we definitely didn't talk about me moving out; and part anger because she wasn't in control of me and everything I do. A good deal of self-pity because I'm treating her so, so wrong and she's done nothing to deserve this kind of treatment, and an even bigger dose of indignation because she's Shae Baker, by God, and she's the one who does the leaving. My stomach twists at the thought of her reaction, and I hate myself a little bit for caring at all.

"You see, that look right there is why you need to leave." My twin sister, Willa, is pointing her finger in my face. "Do *not* feel sorry for that gaslighting bitch. You are taking what's yours and getting out. This is what you want, remember?"

"Yes, it absolutely is. It's just—"

Willa puts her fingers on my lips. "I'm gonna stop you right there." Her face softens and she pulls me into a hug. "I know this is hard, which is why I'm doing it and not you." She pulls away and holds me at arm's length. "Go to the Dew Drop Inn and stake it out to make sure Shae doesn't leave early. I'm guessing the guys and I need about two hours to be cleared out of here. I'll text you when we're done, OK?"

I take a deep breath. "OK, yes. You're right. You're right. You're absolutely right."

One corner of Willa's mouth quirks up at the nod to the *When Harry Met Sally* quote. Carrie Fisher's Marie was as delusional about her married boyfriend as I've been about Shae Baker for the last five years.

Like all good love stories, it started out idyllic. Shae was charming and suave and so confident. In charge, but not in an overbearing way. Handsome and sexy, and the sex was next-level amazing. She wanted to take care of me, and I desperately wanted to be taken care of. It was nice to come home to someone who would manage our house, social engagements, vacations, bills. Our life, basically. It helped that we were both career-driven, had the same taste in decor, loved to travel, and enjoyed the company of the same friends. Mostly. Slowly, managing our life morphed into Shae managing *my* life. What I thought were mutual interests faded from our lives until we were doing things Shae loved and I tolerated. When Shae planned something I didn't want to do, she went without me, but not until she'd tried to manipulate and guilt trip me into going. Until one Saturday night I was alone at home, again, I realized that it had been weeks since we'd gone out together and I didn't care. I was relieved when she wasn't around.

That was the first night I smelled another woman on her.

I'm done.

"I love you," I say to Willa.

"Well, you ought to because I'm amazing."

I roll my eyes, but can't help smiling. Willa is the sunshine in my life. The yin to my yang. Not only my sister but my best friend. Confidante. We finish each other's sentences and, honestly, we don't even have to speak most of the time to know what the other person wants or is going to say. Is it any wonder we've both had such hard luck with romantic partners when we have someone in our life who fills that emotional role?

"And so humble, too," I tease.

"You're better at humility than I am. Go." Willa turns me around and gently pushes me toward the door.

I steel myself and walk out the door of the apartment I shared with Shae for four years without a backward glance.

I sit in my car outside the Dew Drop Inn and watch in my rearview mirror as a steady stream of Denver's queer community file into the only lesbian bar in the city. The only lesbian bar in seven hundred miles, to be precise. Dewey's is always packed, but especially on Friday nights for karaoke and the midnight drag show. Shae is a regular on Friday, and a regular on stage. With her lean build, short dark hair, androgynous style, and deep alto voice, she gives the Elvis and James Dean drag kings a run for their money. It was incredibly sexy when she sang songs like "Love Me Tender" to me. Shae would needle me about getting up there and singing to her (I do have a rather nice voice, if I do say so myself), but there is a huge difference between getting up to give a presentation to hundreds of people at work and singing in front of a bar crowd. The first is easy; the idea of the latter makes me want to crawl in a hole and hide. Shae wouldn't let it go, so I stopped going.

Of course, skipping karaoke night meant I no longer got to see or fantasize about the sexy DJ, Toni D, either.

I sit up straight in my seat. "Speak of the devil," I murmur.

Toni strides across the parking lot, greeting people in line with hugs and lots of laughter, and is waved in by the bouncer at the door. No one standing in line seems to care she skipped ahead.

I'm almost tempted to give up my stakeout and go inside so I can watch her all night, maybe find the courage to talk to her for the first time, see if this secret attraction I've been harboring for a couple of years can withstand an honest to goodness conversation.

I slouch down in my seat. I'm here to stake out Shae, not flirt with another woman in front of her. Plus, the last thing I need to do is start cruising for women. The idea of getting back out there, trying to make a connection, getting to know someone again is exhausting. I just don't have the energy or mental bandwidth for it right now. I shudder at the thought of dating apps.

I glance in my rearview mirror and see her, Shae, looking gorgeous, strutting across the parking lot with four of our friends and a young, beautiful woman on her arm. Even though my mind knows better, my stomach and heart clench at the sight. I'm not sure if it's from seeing Shae with her arm around a much younger and hotter version of myself, or our four friends with her, laughing at whatever Shae is saying and apparently not caring at all that she is cheating on me, since we haven't technically broken up. As far as Shae knows, Willa and I are in Texas having Thanksgiving with our mother. As if we'd ever do that willingly.

Shae palms the woman's ass as the door to the bar closes behind them.

"That fucking bitch," I say to the empty car, my blood boiling. I already know she's been cheating on me, but the least she could do is sneak around. But she's right out here in public, at Dewey's, with her hands all over another woman's ass. And our friends just go along with it.

"Jesus, I'm such an idiot." Harmonicas wail out of my car's

Bose speakers, reminding me of the epic fuck-you break-up album of my youth.

I know exactly what I'm going to do.

I turn my car off and launch myself out the door before I can change my mind.

CHAPTER TWO

TONI

I see her as soon as she walks in the door, which is saying something with the crush of queer people crammed into the bar. She looks like a CEO on casual Friday—dark skinny jeans, Chelsea boots, a black blazer and a sky-blue silk shirt underneath. Tasteful jewelry. Hair pulled back into a tight ponytail.

I'm immediately turned on.

She catches my eye and stops for a moment, before continuing through the crowd, her gaze never leaving mine.

I don't know her name—it starts with an A, I think—but I've seen her here at the Dew Drop Inn a few times with her girlfriend, Shae (with an e). Whenever she isn't here Shae makes at least one trip to the bathroom with whatever woman in the bar has a passing resemblance to the CEO, if she didn't bring the doppelgänger with her.

"Audrey's finally had enough, I see," Max says in her bored-with-the-world deadpan voice.

"Who?" I ask.

Max scoffs. "The woman you're tractor-beaming toward you with your fuck-me eyes."

"I'm not looking at her like that."

"Sure."

Audrey. It suits her perfectly. How could I have forgotten it?

And suddenly, Audrey pops out at the front of the stage, which is a one-step platform crammed in the corner. She's a little breathless. She lifts her chin to meet my gaze.

Of course I know she's pretty—I might have stared at her more than a few times when I'm in town and DJ karaoke nights at Dewey's—but I've never been this close to her. Her skin is pale and flawless, though her cheeks are flushed from the heat of so many bodies packed into a tiny space. Her makeup is subtle, her lips a glossy dark pink. Dark eyebrows contrast with her blond hair. Audrey had always been the quiet one at the table, laughing at her girlfriend's jokes, blushing on more than a few occasions each night, grimacing when Shae got too tight, never giving in to her entreaties to sing on karaoke night. The Audrey standing in front of me though isn't reserved, but fierce and determined. There's fear in her expression, too. My gut clenches and a strange feeling of protectiveness comes over me.

She inhales deeply, as if mustering the courage to get on the stage, or maybe to speak at all.

"Can I go first?" she asks. Her voice is smooth as warm honey.

You can do anything you want, I think, but thankfully don't say. In fact, I don't say anything. I've apparently lost the ability to speak.

"Sure," Max says.

Audrey smiles at Max. A stab of jealousy wakes me up.

"What song do you want?" I ask.

One side of Audrey's mouth quirks up, and she looks mischievous. My stomach does a little tango.

She steps up onto the stage next to me, leans close, and

purrs into my ear, "The greatest break-up song of all time, Toni D."

Oh good lord in heaven. This woman is going to kill me.

I grin and put one headphone next to my ear. "Let me know when you're ready."

Her grin is full and wicked.

Audrey steps on the stage and I catch a whiff of her perfume, clean with the subtlest hint of spice. She faces the back of the stage, takes off her jacket, and drapes it over a stool, revealing a silk tank and long arms with creamy skin. She releases her honey blond hair from her ponytail, runs her hands through it to give it volume. My heartbeat is racing like a thoroughbred's. This isn't some half-drunk lesbian blowing off steam with a bad rendition of "I Will Survive." This woman means business.

And I am more turned on by the second.

Max nudges me, and nods toward the crowd. "Shae with an E, two o'clock."

Audrey's girlfriend is hot, no doubt about it. Shae is androgynous, tall and thin, with olive skin and perfectly coiffed short dark hair. Audrey and Shae make a striking couple: two stylish, professional lesbians that ooze money. I never bothered to learn too much about Audrey because she is so obviously not my type, not to mention out of my league. I've noticed her watching me from time to time, but I chalked it up to her being fascinated by a dirtbag like me. Fascinated like I'm a bug under a microscope, that is.

Shae hasn't seen Audrey, yet. Neither has the woman draped over Shae's shoulder.

"This is going to be epic," Max says, her usual *I'm bored with everything and everyone* resting bitch face morphed into as close to glee as Max will ever get.

"Hey, hey, hey!" I say to the crowd, not having to force excitement into my voice for once. "Time to prime the pump for the midnight drag show! You aren't going to want to miss this singer, who I have a feeling is about to blow our minds. I know *I* wouldn't want to break her heart. I feel sorry for the poor soul who has. She's about to sing the greatest break-up song ever written. If you don't know what song I'm talking about, you *oughta* know!"

Audrey steps forward into the spotlight, holding the microphone. Shae looks away from Betty Bimbo and her face goes white. One of her friends mouths, "Holy shit," and starts laughing. Audrey sports the biggest *you're goddamned right it's me, bitch* grin I've ever seen. My stomach is somersaulting with excitement. I'm halfway in love with this woman already. The familiar song starts and the entire bar erupts in a cheer.

Audrey's voice is low, sultry, and sexy as she sings the first two lines. She inhales for the next verse and her voice changes from sexy to gravelly and angry and goddamn if she isn't the sexiest woman I've ever seen in my life.

"Shit." Max laughs.

Shae's new girlfriend bristles. Shae with an E looks as turned on as I am, until Audrey changes the words to the song so there is no doubt who she's singing about. The crowd loves it; amid the cheers and claps I hear some *Yas girl!* and *Tell her, sister* and *Preach!*

Audrey is feeling it now. She isn't looking at her ex anymore, but is doing one of the best nineties rocker chick impressions I've ever seen. Eyes closed, bent over rocking to the beat of the music, long hair whipping around her, obscuring her face. I glance at Shae and want to mess up her hair. I've always thought she was a douche and the expression on her face proves it.

"You sing it, baby!" a drag queen calls out. Cheers, hoots, whistles, and more words of encouragement are thrown toward the stage.

Audrey grins and straightens, her voice shifting down to a

sultry level. The bar has quieted in anticipation, knowing that in a few seconds the sexy rocker chick is going to be unleashed again. If every pair of panties in this bar aren't soaking, I'm not a lesbian.

"If *you* don't fuck her tonight, I'm going to," Max says.

"Don't be crude, Max."

At the bridge, Audrey turns around, eyes closed, and sways to the music. She is absolutely lost in it, and the expression of joy on her face is something to behold. When the music starts to change, she opens her eyes and they meet mine. She winks at me, turns around, and brings the song home.

When she finishes, the bar is silent for a couple of beats, before every person in the place, save Shae and the new girl-friend, goes crazy. Audrey lifts her arms and takes in the adulation, a smile on her face, her eyes shining. She's free. Her gaze lands on her ex, who's moving toward the stage. Audrey puts the mic up to her mouth.

"Stop right there. You've had your way, now I've had my say. Fuck you." She holds the mic out and drops it, turns on her heel, and exits through the back door next to the stage.

The bar erupts into the biggest cacophony of cheers I've ever heard at Dewey's, with plenty of jeers for Shae with an E thrown in. A quick glance at the crowd and I grin. The new girl-friend is gone.

I see Audrey's jacket on the stool and grab it. I turn to Max. "I'm going to try to catch her. Whatever you do, don't let Shae follow her outside," I tell Max.

"Are you coming back?"

"Hopefully not," I say, grinning. "You good?"

"Sure, no problem," Max says. "I'll just DJ on top of everything else I have to do tonight."

"Thanks, Max. I owe you one."

"I'll add it to the list."

I rush out into the chill November night. Hell, I would have followed her even if she hadn't left the coat. I spot her walking around the corner of the bar toward the street, her arms wrapped around herself against the cold. I call out and she stops by a black Mercedes.

When I reach her, I'm breathless. "You forgot this."

She takes it from me and steps back. "Thank you." Her voice is small, and she sniffs at the end. All of her bravado from moments ago is gone. I step closer. The need to comfort her is overwhelming, and I'm not the comforting type. At least I never have been. It stops me in my tracks.

"Are you OK?"

"Am I OK? Good question." She puts on the jacket and sniffs again.

"You were amazing in there."

She looks away. "I just made a complete fool of myself, but thank you."

"What?" I step closer. "Every woman in that bar fell in love with you tonight. If you really want to make Shae with an E jealous, you should go back in there and let them fight over who takes you home."

She narrows her eyes, and scoffs. "That's not why I did it."

"I know, I didn't mean to... that was a stupid thing to say. I'm sorry. But you should have heard the crowd when you left. They were letting Shae with an E have it." I put my hands in my pockets for warmth. I forgot my coat, too.

There is an awkward silence, and Audrey looks around nervously. "I should go. I don't want *Shae with an E* coming to find me."

"So, you call her that, too?"

Audrey laughs again. "No, but it's perfect. It's always annoyed me, the way she introduces herself." She reaches for her car door.

I'm desperate to keep her here, but I have no idea what to say.

"Um, hey. Do you want to go grab a cup of coffee?" I blurt. I might be charming, but I've never been suave.

"Don't you have karaoke night to DJ?"

"Max gave me the night off." Not exactly a lie.

"When?"

"Um, earlier." Three minutes ago is technically earlier.

Audrey tilts her head. "Are *you* trying to take me home, Toni D?"

"No. NO. Not at all. I just, well I saw your expression when you came up to the stage and I thought you might want to talk. Unless you have a friend to talk things out with. You probably do. Of *course* you do. I, um, yeah, I'm sorry. I can see how you would think I'm hitting on you. I wouldn't do that."

"Oh, really? Why not?" She crosses her arms over her chest as if she's offended.

I open my mouth, then shut it. Does Audrey *want* me to hit on her? I decide to play it safe, turn it into a joke. "For the record, I'm not that kind of girl."

Audrey laughs again. "I've seen you pick up plenty of women over the years to know *that's* a lie."

"Oh, so you've watched me?"

"You're hard to miss since you're the DJ." Audrey studies me, then her eyes glance over my shoulder. I follow her gaze and see Shae rounding the corner. "Get in," Audrey says.

I scramble to get into the low-slung two-door coupe. The door closes with the soft whump only luxury cars make. Shae knocks on the window, walking backward as Audrey backs out of the spot.

"Come on, Audie. Let's talk. I'm sorry."

Audrey stops the car, puts it in drive, and gives her ex-girl-friend the finger before she floors it. The tires squeal and the car fishtails out of the parking lot.

Audrey is grinning almost manically. "I've always wanted to do that. But it's bad for your tires so I never have."

"A-plus, Vin Diesel." I run my hands along the leather seat and door. "Nice car."

"Thanks."

"It smells like you," I say, and immediately regret it.

"I smell like a new car?"

"No, I mean, your perfume... earlier... and the... um..."

Audrey laughs, and I feel ridiculous. Why can't I find my words?

"What perfume do you wear?" I manage.

"Essential oils. I layer them based on how I'm feeling that day. Tonight, I went for spicy. Did you like it?"

"Yes." Maybe that's the key. Simple words. Simple questions. "What do you do for a living?"

"I'm a business consultant."

"Sounds exciting."

Audrey chuckles. "Making it sound dull is easier than explaining it."

"Maybe you'll explain it on our second date."

Audrey glances at me. "Is this a date? I thought you weren't hitting on me."

I want to knock my head against the dashboard. "No, of course not. I'm talking about the date after the date I'm going to ask you on after we get a completely platonic coffee at that little diner right there." I point down the street at my favorite all-night diner. "I've drunk a lot of coffee and eaten a lot of pancakes at Annie's. Breakfast for dinner is my favorite meal."

"Mine, too. How did you know I was driving to Annie's?"

"I'm a mind reader, didn't you know?"

Audrey parks, turns off the car. Her eyes settle on mine. "You're definitely not a mind reader." She opens her door and steps out.

"How do you know?"

She leans back into the car and, with that sexy mischievous grin I already adore, she says, "Because if you were you'd know I'm not thinking about eating pancakes." She shuts the door and heads to the diner door.

And now my tomboy briefs are destroyed.

CHAPTER THREE

AUDREY

Did I *seriously* just imply to Toni that I want to go down on her? If Toni's darkened eyes, slightly gaping mouth, and searching expression when she settles into the booth are any indication then yes, yes I did.

Who in the world *am* I tonight?

My only excuse is that I'm still riding the adrenaline high from being on stage. I can't believe I sang to a bar full of people. Not only sang but rocked out. I think about all the times I sat in the audience with Shae, embarrassed for the singers who were, by and large, terrible. Watching them makes my palms sweat and my heart race, and why in the world would I want to sit through hours of torture every single week? So, I avoided karaoke nights as much as possible. I occasionally went to make Shae happy, and to disturb her plans to take her latest side piece. But mostly I went to see Toni. I've lusted after her for a while, though before tonight she never gave me a second glance. And, despite what Toni said, I'm sure I looked ridiculous up there, but what's done is done. Thank God Willa wasn't there to see it. I'd never live it down.

My phone buzzes. Speak of the devil.

Willa 11:34 p.m. *All clear.*

That's my cue to stop surveilling Shae and meet Willa at our new townhome. But coffee with Toni is too good to pass up. I text Willa that I'm going to be late. She'll understand. There's also a text from Shae.

Shae 10:15 p.m. *I always knew you should get up on stage. You were amazing. Call me so we can talk.*

I shake my head, put my phone in airplane mode, and stuff it in my purse. Not gonna happen, Shae with an E.

I look at Toni and smile. God, she's young, gorgeous, and completely not my type, physically at least. She's earthy and real, with curly dark hair that is constantly flying out of whatever ponytail or braid she's wearing at the time, and she's always dressed as if she might run across a hiking trail and wants to be prepared.

As gorgeous as she is, though, what's drawn me to her, has made me brave a few hours of horrible singing every so often, is her charisma. There's no other word for it. Quick with a smile and a laugh, Toni always struck me as someone who would be, well, *fun*. Shae, for all her intelligence and sophistication, is not fun.

So, here I am. Suddenly nervous about finally having a conversation with Toni because I'm not an idiot. She was hitting on me back at the bar. Who am I to turn down the attentions of a beautiful woman? It's not like it will go anywhere. We'll flirt a little (I hope), eat our breakfast for dinner, and say goodbye. Maybe exchange numbers. The last thing I need, or want, is to start dating someone right now.

"Is Toni short for anything?" I ask, jumping right in with the stupidest question imaginable.

Toni is staring at me with an expression that sends a rush of blood south. She drapes one arm across the back of the booth. Her forearm is toned and tanned, and my mouth waters at the thought of what the rest of her arm looks like. I haven't had definition like that on my arms in... well, never. I lick my lips, hope Toni doesn't see, and am thankful when the waitress brings us coffee so I can pretend my mouth is watering for that and not this sporty young woman sitting across from me dressed like a mountain guide. I cross my legs and hope my face isn't turning red.

Get a grip, Audrey.

"Antonia. My dad's from Italy. Mom's from Germany. Italian first name, German last name. My sister got the reverse."

"Different last names? That must have been difficult during school."

"Eh, not really. We grew up in a small community and everyone knew us. How 'bout you? Named after Audrey Hepburn?"

"Guilty as charged."

Toni nods with a small smile on her face.

"I look nothing like her."

"No, you're more beautiful than she is. Your name fits you."

I hate blushing because I don't blush so much as blotch. From the burning on my face, I know I am blotching from forehead to neck. "How do you figure that?"

"You're classically beautiful. A bit reserved. Not standoffish, not into meaningless chitchat."

"Hmm," I say, not wanting to admit how on the nose she is. About the chitchat. Not that first part. "How could you possibly know anything about me when we spoke for the first time thirty minutes ago?"

"I've noticed you," Toni says.

My stomach flutters in a way it hasn't in years. "Hmm," I hum again, and sip my coffee. This is news to me. Very pleasant news. My gaze keeps wandering to that arm draped over the back of the booth and now it's wandering down her firm forearm and to her hands. Strong hands. Fingers that make me wan—

"What kind of consultant are you?" Toni asks.

I meet Toni's eyes and she's grinning, her eyebrows lifted. Busted. I clear my throat.

"Operational. I help businesses reorganize and update their policies and processes to be more efficient and cost effective."

Toni closes her eyes and snores loudly.

I laugh. "Exactly. Sometimes I feel the same way. But my work is project based and I'm starting a new project on Monday. Actually, it's my first project as a consultant."

"Really? What made you decide to go that route?"

I grimace, not sure why I opened this conversational door. But Toni's expression is open and guileless. She's curious, but I can tell if I drew a line, she wouldn't press me. Somehow, this makes me want to tell her everything.

"I was passed over for a promotion, a big one." Toni lifts her eyebrows, intrigued. "It was politics. I'd blown the whistle on an inter-office affair the year before. Not getting the role was payback, apparently."

Toni leans forward. "You could sue them for that, couldn't you?"

I shrug. "They promoted a woman who was qualified, just not as good as I am. It would be a hard case to prove. Besides, I'm really excited about this next chapter."

"Big changes personally and professionally, huh?"

I chuckle. "Yeah. Might as well blow up my life all at once. So," I say, wanting to stop talking about me. "Did you do your Christmas shopping today?"

Toni scoffs. "God no. I avoid retail at all costs, and retail on Black Friday? Seventh circle of hell for me."

I laugh. "I hate shopping, except going to the grocery store."

"Ugh. I hate all forms of shopping. Which is why I never have anything worth eating in the apartment."

"What do you do for a living?"

For all my admiration of Toni I'd never asked anyone about her. As soon as I showed any curiosity about a woman, Shae's antenna would have been up.

"I'm a dirtbag."

"Obviously."

Toni smiles, but as I stare at her without smiling, she furrows her brows. The waitress arrives and asks for our order. I order a short stack of buttermilk pancakes and Toni orders eggs, bacon, *and* pancakes.

"I'm an outdoor guide. *That* kind of dirtbag."

"I knew what you meant. But the expression on your face when you thought I didn't was priceless."

Toni relaxes and smiles. "Well, you *did* make the comment about how many women I pick up."

I wave my hand. "I don't judge that. I haven't always been in a relationship, you know. How did you get into guiding?"

"I grew up in the mountains. Skiing in the winter, hiking in the summer. I started guiding when I was young, with my dad. Eventually I led my own tours. I've been doing it ever since. I love being outside, which is why I've resisted taking over from my parents. It's a bunch of paperwork and I'm going to hate it, but my family thinks it's time I join the family business properly. And Mom and Dad want to transition from semi-retired to fully retired." Toni shrugs. "I'll still be a guide, but only as a fill-in, and there is always the weekend."

"Good point."

"I'm definitely not going to be a workaholic like my sister. Are you a workaholic?"

"Sometimes it comes with the job, unfortunately. That's why my sister and I decided to start our own consultancy business, so we could take the jobs we wanted, for companies we believe in, and if we want to take a month off between projects, we can."

"Good for you." Toni drubs her fingers on the table. "Do you want to talk about it? Your ex and singing and all that? I did come here to talk, to be an ear if you need one, not to pick you up."

"How disappointing," I say, staring straight into Toni's hypnotic blue eyes.

"I wouldn't object if it led to that, of course," she clarifies.

"Hmm," I say again. "Your eyes are beautiful."

"Thank you." She smiles politely, as if she's heard this compliment a thousand times before, and she probably has, but I mean my God. Her eyes are a clear, bright blue and framed by long, dark eyelashes and dark brows. With her olive skin, dark curly hair, and strong jaw, Toni is nothing short of striking. Complimenting her eyes is low-hanging fruit, I know, but I can't very well tell her I want to trace the muscles in her forearm with the tip of my tongue, now, can I?

No, really. Could I tell her that?

No. I used up my reserve of courage on that stage tonight, and implying I wanted to go down on her.

I clear my throat. "I heard Alanis Morissette on the radio and I remembered listening to her album when it first came out, all that rage and anger on full display, with no apologies. I remembered how empowered I felt listening to it and I wondered where my empowerment went. In my personal life, at least. I've been thinking about it for a couple of months, but never thought I'd get the courage."

"Well, you sure picked a good night for it. Go big or go home."

I chuckle and watch as I twist my mug around on the table. "I'm just glad it's over."

Toni hums noncommittally.

"What?" I asked.

"Are you sure Shae won't be waiting at home to beg you to take her back?"

"She's already texted me. Somehow taking credit for how well I did on stage tonight. I ignored it. She'll arrive home to a half-empty apartment. My sister and four moonlighting firemen just moved my stuff out and into our new place."

"So you weren't waffling for those two months, you were planning."

I grin and shrug one shoulder before sipping my coffee.

"My sister would totally do that, too."

"Oh, Willa wants to do much more than humiliate Shae. She wants to punch her in the face."

"Could she?"

I laugh. "She's scrappy and got the attitude to match, so yeah, probably."

"She sounds awesome."

"She would agree. So do I. Are you close with your sister?"

"Not as close as I'd like to be. We're very different and have never quite met the other's expectations."

I never know how to respond when I hear about sisters who don't get along well. I twist my mug on the table, trying to think of something to say before the silence stretches too long. "I liked your Halloween costume last year," I blurt.

"The construction worker?"

I nod.

Toni laughs and says, "Yeah. I've been dressing as the members of the Village People for the last four years. This year I was the biker."

"Oh," I say. I lick my lips and shift in my seat at the visuals rolling through my head. Somehow, I get the courage to look Toni in the eyes. "I'm sorry I missed that."

Toni's eyes darken. "It was popular, for sure."

We hold eye contact for a very long time.

"I just pull things from the closet," she adds.

"Your biker-chick drag is hanging in your closet?"

"It is."

"Waiting to be worn again."

"It is."

"Hmm."

This isn't like me, to be so forward, so suggestive. I've never been a great flirter, but if the expression on Toni's face is any indication, I'm doing something right. The silence between us is full of sexual tension, a pull I haven't felt in a very, very long time. And the eye contact, my God. I refuse to be the one to look away first.

Toni is good at this. Very, very good.

I wonder what Toni is like in bed. What she would let me do...

I'm jarred out of my thoughts when the waitress puts our plates in front of us. We thank her and eat. I barely taste my pancakes and don't see my food at all. My mind is on other things. I can't bring myself to meet Toni's gaze again, sure she will see every thought written on my face.

"What do you do when you aren't working?" Toni asks.

"I've spent most of the last ten years working, climbing the corporate ladder. It didn't leave much free time." I cut a square out of the center of my pancakes and spear it on my fork. I take a bite of my pancakes, soaked through with fresh butter and warm syrup, and groan. I open my eyes and Toni is watching me, her mouth slightly open, her eyes dark, and I know all I have to do is ask to get what I want. "I hope that working for myself will give me more free time for... extracurricular activities."

Toni raises an eyebrow and starts to eat again. "What kind of extracurricular activities do you think you'll be participating in?"

"Yoga. Reading. Photography."

"Hiking?"

"I'm not much of a hiker."

Toni leans back and grasps her chest. "Right through the heart," she says.

I laugh. "I'm not a complete couch potato. I like to kayak."

"White water?" Toni asks, hope in her voice.

"More like a calm lake in the middle of the city at sunrise."

"Well, it's better than nothing, I guess," Toni says. "You know, I can help you with your hiking aversion."

"Can you?"

"Yes, I'm a professional, you know. One of the best in my field."

"Oh are you?"

"Absolutely. I've climbed every fourteener in the state."

My fork clatters on my plate. "Seriously?"

"Yep."

"You've climbed all fifty-eight peaks over fourteen thousand feet in Colorado? I mean, I know people do that, I've just never met one."

Toni laughs. "We're a strange breed, no doubt. I've been hiking since I was two. It's not that big of an accomplishment, though I did beat my sister's record as the youngest to complete them all by a month."

"How old were you?"

"Eleven."

"Eleven?"

"My record was broken later that year. But I'll always be above my sister in the record books."

"Wow."

"Don't worry, I won't take you on a fourteener for a while."

I laugh. "You'll never get me on a fourteener, Toni."

"Never say never."

She wiggles her eyebrows, and I laugh again.

"Thank you for making me laugh," I say.

"You have a wonderful laugh."

A pleasant warmth starts in my stomach and spreads through me. "Thank you."

Toni leans over the table. "I have a confession to make."

I swallow. "Oh? About what?"

"I've wanted you since I saw you walking through the bar."

I give her what I hope is a mischievous smile. "And I left my jacket hoping you would follow me."

Toni licks her lips. "Wanna get out of here?"

I could draw this out, flirt a little more, tease her, but why? I want her as much as she wants me. I motion to the waitress for our check.

CHAPTER FOUR

TONI

I open the door to the apartment and peek inside. It's mostly clean, and it'll have to do. Audrey steps close and puts her chin on my shoulder.

"What are you doing?" she whispers.

Energy hums between us like an electric current. I wonder if Audrey feels it too.

"Checking to make sure my snake is in its cage," I whisper.

Audrey jumps back. I meet her horrified expression with a grin. She narrows her eyes.

"You don't have a snake."

"Hate the little fuckers."

When the door closes behind us, Audrey pushes me against it and presses her body into mine.

"Someone ate their Wheaties this morning," I say.

"Take me to your bedroom. Now," she growls.

I meet Audrey's heated gaze. "I take it you want to be in charge?"

"Yes," she says on a shaky breath.

That little peek of insecurity makes me want to fold her in my arms. "OK. Whatever you want."

Audrey inhales sharply and her eyes darken. She leans forward, and I close my eyes, anticipating a kiss. Instead, her lips brush my ear again.

"I told you to take me to your bedroom."

On trembling legs, I lead Audrey by the hand down the hall. She closes the door behind us and leans against it. She leers at me, there's no better word, her gaze raking up and down my body, and licks her lips. She is one hundred percent objectifying me and I am here for it.

"Come here." Her voice is soft, but firm and sure.

I stand in front of her and raise my eyebrows. I have absolutely no idea what she wants, what she's going to demand next, and I am so keyed up in anticipation that I must force myself to not bounce on the balls of my feet.

Audrey steps close, so close I can feel her breath against my lips. Her gaze rakes over my face. One hand reaches up and strokes my cheek and her finger pulls my bottom lip down. I take a deep shuddering breath. It is all I can do not to return her touch, to keep my arms at my sides when all I want to do is wrap myself around this sexy woman and pull her close.

Audrey reaches behind me and pulls my long braid over my shoulder. With deft fingers and an unwavering gaze, she undoes my braid. I tug her ponytail free and her hair pours through my fingers like threads of silk. Audrey fluffs my dark curls. I know exactly how wild my hair looks—I wear it in a braid most of the time for a reason—and by the expression on Audrey's face she is incredibly turned on by it.

"I've wanted to see your hair like this for months," she says quietly.

"You have?"

"I saw you with it down once for a split second before you put it back up."

I smile and hope it doesn't look as cocky as I feel. "You *have* noticed me."

Audrey chuckles. "You're the only reason I go to karaoke, Toni."

"Oh."

"Yes, *oh*," Audrey says.

Since we walked through the apartment door, her voice has dropped into a sultry alto, the stuff of fantasies and wet dreams. My tomboy shorts are soaked, my clit throbbing in anticipation of Audrey's touch.

"I've wanted to do this for a while, too," she purrs. She kisses me, gently. Her lips are as smooth and silky as her hair, and she wastes no time sliding her tongue inside my mouth. We pull each other close and fall into the kiss. It's slow and sensual and erotic, and as much as I want Audrey to touch me, as much as I want my lips to map every inch of her body, I could spend the entire night kissing her and it would still be the best night of my life.

"Wow," she says when we finally pull apart.

"Yeah, wow," I say. "I... um..." I can't find words for the emotions racing through my body, my heart, my mind, so I pull her in for another kiss, push her blazer from her shoulders, and let it drop to the floor. "Oh my God your skin is so soft," I say, running my hands down her bare arms.

"Undress for me."

"Do you want me to take my time, make a production of it? Or get to it?"

Audrey raises an eyebrow.

"Get to it. Right," I say. "Um, before we go any further, I'm tested regularly and it's all good. Healthy as a horse. I can show you the results if you like."

"I believe you. I've been tested regularly since I discovered Shae's problem with monogamy. All clear."

"I have dams, too. If you'd like to use them."

Audrey chuckles, her gaze sliding down my body to my

center. She bites one corner of her lip and raises her gaze to meet mine. "No, thanks. But you can."

I step forward and pull Audrey to me. "I know this kind of discussion can ruin the mood a bit," I whisper.

Audrey brushes my hair out of my face. "I think consent is sexy. It makes me want you more."

I kiss her hard, and let my hands roam her clothed body down to her ass. I pull her into me and bend her back slightly as my tongue slides into her warm mouth. Her hands are in my hair, and she moans. I'm taking charge a bit, but Audrey doesn't seem to mind.

She pulls away and says, "I could kiss you all night."

"Same."

"But, while we're doing it, let's fuck, too."

I grin. "Even better."

"Now. Get undressed."

I try to undress as gracefully and quickly as possible, but my clothes don't cooperate. There are too many buttons on my shirt (where are snaps when I need them?), too many hooks on my boots (always a pain in the ass), and my zipper gets stuck (God's just laughing at me now). When I finally step out of my jeans and stand in only my sports bra and boy shorts, Audrey is close, a mischievous grin on her face.

"Would you like some help with the rest?" she teases, one finger sliding up and down the front zipper of my sports bra.

"If that means your hands will finally be on my body, then yes."

"Hmm." Her fingers trace along my sides and across my abdomen as she circles behind me. "Like this?" she whispers in my ear.

"Um, yes. This is good."

She unzips my bra and it slides off and drops to the floor. It's Audrey's turn to explore my arms, and I can't help but flex them for her. She chuckles into my ear, low and throaty. "You saw me drooling over your forearms earlier, didn't you?"

"Nooo," I say.

"I'm an arm girl, what can I say?" She lifts my arm and with an open mouth and soft, warm tongue, kisses my bicep. I barely have time to register how phenomenal that simple kiss feels when her free hand finds my nipple and squeezes it gently. "I also like breasts," she whispers. "And necks." She kisses my neck. "And ears." She kisses my ear. "You taste amazing, Toni. I thought you might."

My head drops back on her shoulder, and she kisses up and down my neck and along my shoulder.

"I had no idea you would be a talker," I say.

"Do you mind?" She breathes the question into my ear in her low, honeyed voice and my knees almost buckle.

"God, no," I croak.

Still behind me, Audrey's hands slide down my sides, taking my briefs down to the floor. I kick them out of the way, and she places a kiss on my ass that makes me shudder from its unexpectedness.

"Do you like that?" she asks.

I nod vigorously and moan something unintelligible.

As she stands, she scrapes her fingernails gently up my legs. Her hands move across my abs to the triangle of hair between my legs. Her fingers rake through the top of my curls, and she purrs in my ear. "Nice."

I whimper because I literally can't form words right now.

I'm not sure what I expected from Audrey, but this amount of confidence, sensuality and sexiness was not it.

"Audrey," I groan. "Please."

"Please what?" Her fingers skirt dangerously close to my clit. I raise my hips, hoping to feel her touch, but she pulls her fingers away.

"Um..."

"Please finish you?"

"Yes."

"Or please tease you mercilessly until all I have to do is ask you to come and you will, without touching you at all." She bites my shoulder and pinches my nipple.

My entire body jerks, a heady mix of pain and pleasure coursing through every inch of me.

"You are very close, aren't you?"

"God, yes."

"Hmm," she hums into my ear. "I can't wait to watch you come, but first, I want to feel your skin against mine. Undress me." She nips my earlobe, and my knees nearly buckle beneath me.

It isn't easy, I'm not going to lie. I'm trembling with desire, and my fingers have forgotten how to grasp the hem of her tank and pull it over her head. Audrey unhooks her bra and tosses it aside, and my mouth waters at the sight of her full breasts and hardened nipples. My body thrums with the need to touch Audrey, to kiss between her breasts, to take them into my mouth, to feel Audrey's hand on my head, arching her back and pushing her breasts deeply into my mouth.

"I'll eventually let you do everything you're thinking right now after I get my fill of you," Audrey says, and licks her lips.

"Jesus Christ," I say, and nearly come on the spot.

Audrey blesses me with another wicked grin before her lips meet mine. It's tender and gentle, and she runs her tongue lightly against my lips, asking for more, not demanding. My heart hammers in my chest as Audrey takes possession of my mind and body with the sexiest kiss I've ever received. The throbbing between my legs is insistent, demanding to be sated.

I pull away, panting, flushed, desperate. "You are sexy and gorgeous and as much as I love everything you're doing and saying if you don't fuck me soon, I'm going to explode."

She pulls me close, our bodies fitting together perfectly, and crashes her lips against mine. I open completely, and let Audrey take whatever she wants. Audrey tastes so good, I cannot wait to taste the rest of her. Her fingernails scratch down my back. I shudder with pleasure and pain.

She gently pushes against my chest, and I fall back on the bed.

CHAPTER FIVE

AUDREY

A smile of anticipation lights up Toni's gorgeous face. She's into me being in charge.

So am I.

Her hair is an explosion of curls, dark against the white pillow. She's lean but muscular, with multiple tan lines of varying shades on her biceps, shoulders, collarbones, and thighs. I remember the fantasies of this identical scenario I've had over the last few years and am trying to decide if I should kiss my way up her long, toned legs, or if I should go right to her perfect tits, when Toni slides her feet up the bed, tenting her legs, her calves shielding my view of her. She places her hands on her knees, and I lick my lips in anticipation. When she doesn't move, our eyes meet.

"You're in charge, remember?" she says.

Sexual power surges through me, something I haven't felt in a very long time. My heart races with the realization Toni wants me bad enough to offer herself to me, to do exactly what I want, without a clue of what that entails. Is that trust, or lust?

Let's see, shall we?

"Spread your legs for me," I say. I mean it to come out

authoritative, but it comes out raw and rough, and my voice breaks on the word *me*. My comfort zone is a tiny speck in the rearview mirror. Even before Shae, who wanted me to be a pillow princess, I wasn't a domineering or demanding lover. But there's something about Toni that puts me at ease. Somehow, I know that with Toni I'm safe showing this side of me, one I didn't even realize lurked beneath my admittedly strait-laced exterior.

When Toni spreads her legs, I stop breathing.

The dark curls between her legs are soaked, her lips are wet and swollen open in invitation. I might have gasped because Toni props herself on her arms.

"What's wrong? Do you not like, um, natural?"

I pull my eyes away and meet her worried gaze.

"No, it's not that, it's just..." I swallow, not sure what I should tell her, what words I can use to convey that I haven't had a woman open up to me like this in years. It's intimate in a way I wasn't expecting. I feel vulnerable and afraid.

And very, very turned on.

I hold her gaze for a long time, and my feelings of vulnerability ratchet up to about a fifteen on a scale of ten. I decide for simplicity and a bit of crudeness, to get us back on the track of a meaningless one-night stand.

I'm still standing at the end of the bed. "I can smell you from here."

It's absolutely not a lie, but it's not something I've ever said in my life. What the hell is this woman doing to me? And why do I feel more like myself than ever before?

"What do you expect with you standing there looking like Botticelli's Venus come to life," Toni says.

My mouth drops open.

"I'm not *just* a sexy mountain woman, you know." She slides her hand between her legs, moistens her fingers, and brings them to her mouth, sucking them inside.

Fuck me, but I want to pounce on her, to bury my head between her legs, drink her in, have my fill. She would probably come instantly and, as satisfying as that would be, I want this to last. God knows when I'll have this chance again. It takes every ounce of willpower I possess to wait, but I suspect the reward will be worth it.

"I wish you could see the expression on your face right now, Audrey." Toni's voice is husky, and it cracks on my name.

"Hmm," I say. I run my hand up my stomach to cradle my breast. Toni licks her lips, and more blood rushes to my center. I've never come while giving a woman an orgasm, but I might tonight.

Sounds like a good goal.

"I wish you could see how delicious your pussy looks," I say, and Toni groans.

I smile; I'm not usually a talker, and I've never been one to talk dirty, but if this is the response I get, maybe I should be. I crawl across the bed between Toni's legs, until I'm hovering over her, but not touching her. Toni lifts her hips, wanting connection.

"Not yet," I say.

"You're killing me, Audrey."

"That's the point," I purr.

"Can I touch you?" I raise an eyebrow and Toni amends her question. "May I touch you, please?"

"Listen to the good little girl's grammar, and so polite. But no."

My breasts hang between us, my nipples tight and erect. I lower myself so that they lightly brush against Toni's, and she gasps.

"Yes, please," she says.

Our gazes lock. I rock back and forth above her, my breasts caressing hers with slow, deliberate strokes. Toni lifts her hands as if to touch me, then lowers them and grips the sheets.

"Do you like being edged, Toni?" I whisper.

"I'm usually the one doing the edging," she says.

Oh my God I can't wait for this woman to fuck me. One thing about Shae, she was an expert at edging, and I loved it. I just hope I learned the technique she used on me for five years.

My hips drop and our centers meet for the briefest of moments, but long enough for me to feel Toni's desire. She lifts her hips to keep the connection, but I rise higher. She emits a frustrated groan but drops her hips obediently.

"Such a good girl," I say, and Toni's nostrils flare. I had no idea I could purr like a femme fatale luring a man to his doom.

My God. I'm turning *myself* on.

"It's very hard for you to be a good girl, isn't it?" I lower my hips and tilt them into Toni and go still. She is hot and wet against me.

Toni closes her eyes and swallows. She licks her lips and opens her eyes. "I want to be good for you."

I smile and reward her with a slow thrust. She tilts her hips and I don't scold her. The new angle feels amazing. Her hair is rough against me, and her hard clit rubs deliciously against mine. I inhale sharply and stop. Now I know for sure that my orgasm is on the edge, ready and waiting for release.

"Do you want to come?" I purr.

Toni nods vigorously.

"If I were nice, I would let you come right now." I lift one arm and touch Toni's neck behind her ear. "I would start here with my lips and kiss a trail down to your collarbone." My finger lightly follows the path I'm narrating while I rock, ever so slightly against her. "I love collarbones, but I especially love the hollow of a woman's throat." My finger circles the indentation a few times.

Toni's breath is labored.

"Next is, of course, your cleavage." My finger slides down between her breasts. I trail my finger up and down her cleavage, across the swell of her breasts, edging closer and closer to her nipple.

My left arm shakes from holding my weight so I give up the finger tease. Thank God, because I need to taste this woman's essence more than I've ever needed anything in my life.

My lips find the hollow behind Toni's ear and start their journey. Toni's hot skin pebbles at the touch of my lips, and she groans. I smile and continue on, my lips and tongue following the path my finger had mapped out across her damp skin. As I move south, Toni's desire paints a trail across my stomach. I take one of her breasts in my mouth and this time the moan is mine. She tastes delicious, salty with sweat and a slight musk from lotion or essential oils, I'm not sure. My opposite hand caresses her other breast while my tongue circles her rock-hard nipple. I suck her breast in my mouth; it's small and perfectly shaped, and fits inside my mouth like a missing puzzle piece. I switch sides and take my time. I've always appreciated a woman's breasts above all other parts of their body and Toni's breasts are a masterpiece. She tilts her hips up again, her non-verbal but not so subtle hint as to what she wants.

"Use your words, Toni," I say.

"Please. I want your mouth on me. I *need* your mouth on me."

"My mouth is on you. You need to be more specific."

I bite her nipple, hard, and she bucks against me.

"Too much?"

"No."

"Tell me if I do something that you don't like, or that makes you uncomfortable."

"Not licking me is making me *very* uncomfortable."

I can't help it, I laugh. "That's by design."

"Yes, I know, and I hate it. But I love it, too. It's very confusing."

I want to watch this woman come. I want to make this

woman come. I thrust hard against Toni's center once, and holy shit, the jolt of desire that runs through me is breathtaking. She groans and her grip on the sheets tightens.

"Audrey, my God," she says.

"I've never been called God before," I say.

It takes a moment for Toni to get the joke, but when she does, she laughs.

"God, please fuck me with your mouth," Toni says.

"Well, when you put it that way."

I kiss my way down her body, marvel at the ridges on her stomach, and promise myself to return and show my appreciation more fully. I settle between her legs, smell her desire. Her clit is visible, hard and erect, and I gasp slightly. Fuck edging. Teasing her is teasing myself and I cannot wait to get my mouth on her. I lick her once and her back arches. When I take her in my mouth and suck, she lifts her hips and presses herself against my face, wanting more. I'm happy to give it to her.

"Yes," she hisses. "Right there. Do not stop what you're doing."

As if I would. Across the expanse of her washboard abs and beautiful breasts, I watch Toni ride my mouth. My senses are being assaulted by her, being consumed by her; the way she tastes, the way she feels, looks, and the quiet sounds she is making have my body humming with desire.

Too soon, she is trembling, ready for release. I swirl my tongue around her clit and she comes, head thrown back against the pillow, back arched. She shudders her release, her mouth open with a silent scream. That won't do at all.

"Say my name," I demand.

She does one better. She raises up and reaches for me. I don't think, I go to her. She grasps the nape of my neck and presses her forehead against mine.

We're panting, eyes locked, and she growls, "Audrey, come with me."

"God, yes," I say.

Sweat glistening on our skin, breath hard and fast, eyes locked, Toni slides her hand down between us.

"You are fucking magnificent," she says.

When her fingers find my clit, the dam breaks. My orgasm hits me hard and fast, and I cry out her name, which sends her over the edge again. She's not quiet this time, letting loose a string of expletives amid my whimpers and moans. I continue to rock against Toni, wanting to prolong the best orgasm of my life as long as possible.

Toni collapses back on the bed and throws her arms above her head. I fall on top of her. Her arms wrap around me for the first time, and she caresses my back. I almost cry at her gentle touch.

"I love being a lesbian," Toni says.

I laugh into her shoulder. Leave it to Toni to lighten a mood that threatened to get sentimental, at least for me. I lift my head and look at her. She's absolutely glowing and has the most adorable smile on her face. There's no arrogance, just an expression of amused joy.

I lean down and whisper in her ear, "Good, because I'm not finished with you yet."

CHAPTER SIX

TONI

"Jesus, Toni." Audrey collapses onto the bed, her head at my feet.

"Was that satisfactory?" I ask.

Audrey laughs. "Um, yeah. Satisfactory. Definitely. Let's go with that."

We lie there for a while, chests heaving. The smell of sex hovers around us like a fog. It's crazy intimate, the tips of our fingers tracing each other's palms. We are sweaty and exhausted and sated. I am tender and sore in all the right places. I'm not sure I'm going to be able to walk tomorrow, to tell the truth. I can't remember the last time I've been fucked so thoroughly. I want to do it again.

And again.

And again.

"Can I get you anything to drink?" I ask. "Or eat?"

Audrey smiles at me. "I'm still catching my breath."

"You need a few minutes before round three starts, I guess."

"As much as I would love to make you come for a fourth time..."

"Ah, you felt that last one, huh?"

"I did, and I'm very flattered. I wasn't even touching you."

"You were sitting on my face. That's touching."

Audrey laughs. "Right."

"I love your laugh."

Audrey's expression softens. "Thank you for making me laugh."

"You're welcome. Thank you for fucking me so thoroughly I might not be able to function tomorrow. And for being the sexiest woman I've ever been with, hands down," I say.

Audrey laughs. "I'm naked, in your bed. You don't have to use a line on me."

"Calling you sexy is no line. You're amazing, Audrey. Your ex is a moron."

"I was a little worried I'd forgotten how to, uh, do all that. Shae never let me top, and only rarely let me touch her. I haven't touched a woman like I touched you in four years and I've never given a woman head like that."

I sit up. Audrey's fair skin is peeking back through the pink flush that has suffused her body for the last however many hours. I've lost track of time. "Seriously?"

Audrey nods.

I don't judge anyone's tastes or sexual proclivities, that's not my place, but not wanting the woman you're attracted to, the woman you love, to touch you is hard for me to get my brain around. But Audrey and Shae's sex life is none of my business. How it made Audrey feel is none of my business. How Audrey feels in *this moment*, which must be an incredibly vulnerable one for her, *is* my business.

I caress her leg. "You were..." I swallow the lump in my throat. "Perfect. Confident but concerned that you were making me feel good, checking in to make sure I wasn't uncomfortable. That's not as common as it should be, and I really appreciate it."

Audrey smiles and squeezes my hand. "Thank you."

"Also, I'm available anytime if you want to get some practice. Try new things."

"Oh, you are?"

"I know, the sacrifices I make. But someone must do it."

Audrey pinches my thigh, gently. "Maybe I'll take you up on that one day. But I really should be going."

I turn around and lie next to her. I run my fingers down the center of her chest, tracing her belly button, see goosebumps pop out on her smooth skin. "I need my fair ups," I say.

"Your what?"

"You aren't into sports, are you?"

"No, though I tried very hard to impress my seventh grade PE coach Ms. Bilderback. Boy could that woman fill out a tracksuit."

"She sounds amazing."

"She was. And she wore this stunning blue eyeshadow." I suppose I make a weird face. Audrey chuckles and continues. "You had to be there."

"Well, 'fair ups' mean I get to bat as many times as you. In this contest, I need to make you come at *least* two more times."

"Need, or want?"

"One and the same."

"You're competitive, then?"

"Very."

"And it's killing you that I won."

"Well, looking at it another way, I came four times, so I won, and I'm just giving you a chance to tie the score. So. Will you stay for a bit?" I'm desperate for her to stay, but I don't know how to say that without scaring her off.

Audrey smiles, but her expression says no. "I really can't. I am *very* late, and my sister is *very* nosy."

"Yeah. OK. Sure. I respect a woman who sets boundaries. Can I call you this week? For our second date?"

Audrey's gaze roams over my face, as if imprinting it in her memories. "Tonight was amazing, and if this was at any other time in my life, I would stay the night. But it's not. It's just not the right time for me to get involved with anyone."

"Sure. Yeah. It's a one-time thing. No harm, no foul."

"Are you sure? Because you don't look it."

I inhale and get ready to lie. I cup Audrey's cheek and swallow down the huge lump in my throat. "I'm fine. I promise."

"OK."

"Maybe we will see each other around."

"We might."

"Pretend we don't know each other. Flirt a little."

"Role-playing, huh?" Audrey's eyes are dancing with mischief.

I shrug. "Could be fun."

"Why do I suspect you've done this before?"

"The only difference this time is you would know I'm doing it."

Audrey raises one eyebrow. It's not much encouragement, but it's enough for me to keep going.

"If you ever want to have a little fun, no pressure or strings, there's a pub around the corner I go to from time to time. The Chicken Head."

Audrey laughs. "What a name. What if you aren't there?"

You could take my number, I think. But Audrey has set the boundary and the idea to exchange numbers, or even last names, needs to come from her.

"Well, that's the chance you'll just have to take, I guess."

Audrey's gaze moves to my lips, and I think she's going to kiss me. Instead, she rises from bed and gets dressed. I put on my briefs and a tank and run my fingers through my hair for something, anything, to keep myself from begging her to stay. When she's dressed, blazer on, hair pulled back into a ponytail again, she looks like a different woman.

"Well."

"I'll walk you out," I offer.

We stand at the door, neither making a move to open it, but not looking at each other. I decide to be an adult, since I'm going to have to be one 24/7 starting Monday.

I take Audrey's hand and meet her gaze. "I hope everything works out for you, Audrey. You're amazing, and I'm not talking about the sex. Not just the sex, anyway. You're an amazing person here"—I tap Audrey's heart—"and here." I tap her temple.

"You hardly know me."

"The way you hardly know me?" I raise my eyebrows.

Audrey nods her head, and chuckles. "Yeah. OK."

"Don't let your ex worm her way back into your life. You deserve so much better. Take care of yourself. Good luck on Monday." Audrey's brows furrow. "Your new job?"

She smiles. "Right. Of course." She crosses her fingers.

I open the door. Audrey leans forward and kisses me softly on the cheek. "Thank you," she whispers.

"For what?" I say softly.

"Being you." She caresses my cheek, and leaves.

CHAPTER SEVEN

AUDREY

I'm about to press my thumb to the lock to open the door to my and Willa's new townhome when the door opens abruptly. Willa stands there, looking frantic and relieved. Her ash-blond hair is haphazardly piled on top of her head in a lazy bun and wispy layers of hair frame her face. The softness of her relief at seeing me doesn't last long. She narrows her eyes and says, "Where the fuck have you been? It's two thirty in the morning."

I push through the door and close it behind us. "Didn't you get my text?" I ask.

"Met a friend. Going to get a bite to eat. Don't wait up."

"So why do you look like you were about to send out the National Guard to look for me?" I say.

"It's two thirty in the morning. You never stay out past midnight."

"My fairy godmother took pity on me and gave me until three a.m. tonight before I turn into a stick in the mud."

"Oh, honey, you're not a stick in the mud. You're more like a deep-set fence post."

"How flattering," I murmur.

Willa isn't wrong. Birth-order stereotypes are spot on with

the two of us. I'm the solid, responsible sister who spends more time than she should worrying about and mothering Willa, even though she's only three minutes younger and doesn't need mothering in the least. Willa is as solid and responsible as I am. She's also charming and vivacious and makes everything look incredibly easy while she methodically checks everything off the to-do list she pretends she doesn't make every night before she goes to bed.

"What are you doing awake, anyway?"

Willa moves out of my way and sweeps her arm across our new living room and kitchen in her best *The Price is Right* hostess impression. "Unpacking."

Our plan had been to use Saturday and Sunday to unpack before our new project begins on Monday. I expected the main floor of our three-story townhome to be full of boxes. Instead, the long rectangular space is almost pristine, and smells of lemon Pledge and Pine-Sol. Boxes are neatly broken down and stashed in the back corner by the stairs that lead to the basement and garage, and my things have been incorporated in with Willa's seamlessly: my favorite chenille throw I snuggle under when watching TV or reading a book; a bright-orange Gluggle Jug I bought on a business trip to London sits on the kitchen counter next to Willa's cookbooks; a half-empty glass of wine is next to an opened bottle of one of my Saint-Émilion Cabernets. I look at Willa and raise an eyebrow.

"Should have been here to stop me." She walks into the kitchen, pulls a wine glass out of the cabinet, and pours me one.

I follow her into the kitchen, my eye catching the bookshelf by the fireplace where my books are crammed a bit haphazardly onto two shelves.

"You can arrange them by the Dewey Decimal System tomorrow," Willa says, reading my mind.

"I'm actually thinking about sorting them by color."

Willa laughs. "Sure you are."

"Thank you so much for doing all this, Willa. You really didn't have to."

She shrugs and holds out the wine glass. "It kept my mind off worrying about you running into Shae and her convincing you to stay."

"I would be offended, but I deserve that."

We clink our glasses together.

"Cheers."

"Cheers," I say.

I close my eyes and let the wine settle on my tongue before it slides down my throat. I inhale with the deep satisfaction of enjoying a good glass of wine and get the barest whiff of Toni on my lips and I am back in her bed, my head between her legs, watching her come undone, back arching and her pressing into me, her hand on my head holding me exactly where she wants me. I feel myself getting turned on thinking about it.

I raise my eyes and meet Willa's shrewd gaze. My smile falls from my face. I hadn't realized until then that I was smiling.

"Have a nice time catching up with your friend?"

The question sounds innocent enough, but this is Willa. My identical twin who can read my every thought and feel my every emotion. I furrow my brows. Surely she can't feel... she doesn't know... I shift on my feet and press my thighs together.

"You just got laid, didn't you?"

"Oh my God." I pause. "Noooo." I draw out that two-letter word into at least five syllables.

Willa laughs. "You so totally did."

"How could you possibly know that?"

"Because you reek of sex."

"How would you know?"

"Low blow. Don't change the subject. Who was it? Do I know her?" Her face darkens, suddenly. "It wasn't Shae, was it?"

"No. Shae strutted into Dewey's with a teenage bimbo on

her arm with Robin, Daphne, Cam, and Lisa following right behind like a row of ducklings following their mother."

"I never liked them. Any of them."

"You were right," I say. I gulp my wine. "I wish I'd listened to you."

Willa sighs and comes around the counter. She takes me in her arms. I put down my wine glass and hug my sister, my best friend, back.

"None of that," she whispers. "The past is the past and you're moving forward. I'm here for you every step of the way. And your therapist. She's with you, too."

"I don't know what I'd do without you," I say.

"That is something you will never have to worry about." She pulls back and holds me at arm's length. "Now, enough about Shae and her gaggle of sycophants. Who is this woman and how was the sex?"

I can't keep the grin from my face, so I take a huge drink of my wine.

"Spill," Willa says.

"Something snapped when I saw Shae walk in that bar," I say. "I didn't mean to end up in this woman's bed." I pause, remembering the kiss Toni gave me as I left, the softness, the promise or hope of something more. I meet Willa's gaze. "But I'm really glad I did."

"That good, huh?"

I let out a long breath. "Oh, yeah," I say, and laugh.

Willa raises her eyebrows. "I want to ask for a play by play, but I know you won't give me one."

I'm not one to share intimate details, even to Willa, but I feel a little giddy from doing two things so out of character and almost spill it all. I catch myself at the last minute.

"No."

Willa raises both eyebrows. "Oh, I'll get it out of you eventually."

"Not a chance." I take a deep drink of my wine and spy myself in the pristine glass double-oven door. I run a hand through my long blond hair. "Good God, I have sex hair."

"Uh-huh," Willa says, her eyebrows raised in anticipation of a nugget of news.

"Not happening, Willa."

"Come on, throw a celibate girl a bone."

"Watch porn," I say.

Willa's eyes widen. "You had porn sex?"

"No." I can't help but laugh. "No." I sigh. "Fine. She let me run the show. I forgot how much I enjoyed that."

"You were the dom?"

"It wasn't S&M, Willa. I was the top."

Willa leans on the counter and rests her chin on her fist, her expression turning thoughtful. "You haven't done that in a while. Was it like riding a bike?"

The memory of riding Toni's face flashes through my mind. I press my lips together to keep from laughing. "You could say that."

Willa's eyes widen. "Oh my God you're getting a visual. And now *I'm* getting a visual."

"I better not be in that visual."

"Ew, gross. No, it's Sandra Bullock and Ryan Reynolds."

"*The Proposal.* Solid choice."

Willa shakes her head. "Enough of that. Back to you."

"No, really. Keep fantasizing about the characters in an oughties rom-com."

"Hey." Willa reaches out and takes my hand. "I'm happy for you. Shocked as hell you picked up a stranger and slept with them, but happy, too. You're a smokeshow, Auds. Denver lesbians are going to be lining up to date you."

"A smokeshow? What is that, like a vaping convention?"

Willa rolls her eyes. "Use your context clues to figure it out."

"Oh, you're calling me *hot*, as in sexy."

"Yes."

"Which means you're calling yourself hot and sexy, too."

Willa straightens and shrugs her shoulders, lifting her wine glass to her lips, and grins. "It's a truth universally acknowledged."

"When are you going to get back out there?"

She sets her wine glass down with a solid click. "You mean picking up strange women for a one-night stand at the Dew Drop Inn? Never."

I open my mouth to clarify, but Willa cuts me off. "I don't want to talk about this, Auds. OK? I'm fine. I don't need a man to make me happy."

"I know that."

"Then stop pushing me to get back out there. I'm having better sex with my bullet vibe and lesbian porn than I ever had with a man. And this is hardly a good time to try to date. We start our first project Monday, remember?"

I finish off my wine and hold out my glass. "Top me up."

Willa pours more for both of us. "Greta Giordani texted me tonight," she says.

"Why? Everything OK?"

"Well, it's Black Friday. Their website was at a crawl and they'd sold out of their bestsellers by noon. They gave out a ton of discount codes to keep the customers happy."

"Waste of money. Fourteener gear is hot right now."

"Even hotter now they're going to have a shortage going into Christmas."

I touch the tip of my nose in agreement. "A private, family-owned company. American made. People will pay full price. Hell, they ought to raise their prices."

"Greta wants to send out a newsletter on Monday, apologizing for the inconvenience and talking about the future."

"Good idea."

"It's going to be full on for a while." Willa raises the empty wine bottle and shakes it. "If we're going to get drunk, tonight's the night."

"None for me. I'm exhausted."

"I bet." Willa picks up our glasses and puts them in the sink. "Don't forget about our appointment with Johan tomorrow morning."

"I remember." I run my hands through my hair.

Willa catches me and raises her eyebrows. "You gonna finally do it?"

I twist my long hair into a bun and hold it there, looking from side to side in the mirror. "Yeah," I say slowly, letting my hair fall back against my shoulders. "I think I am."

CHAPTER EIGHT

TONI

"You did *not* have sex in my bed." Max leans against the doorjamb, arms crossed over her chest. She has dark circles under her eyes and looks completely exhausted.

"Oh, hey," I say, bundling the bedsheets I'd stripped off her bed into a ball and holding them close to my chest. "I didn't expect you home for a while yet."

"It's two thirty in the morning, Tone."

"Is it?"

I'm not sure if it's the sheets I'm holding or if the entire room smells like sex, but what I *am* sure of is that Max is not amused. I shift from foot to foot, the endorphin high I'd been on after the best sex of my life leaching out of me.

Max relaxes and grins. "I'm just fucking with you, Toni."

My body collapses in relief. "Oh thank God. I'm sorry, Max. But I—"

"Couldn't very well tell a woman like Audrey Adams that you're homeless and sleeping on my couch. I get it."

Adams. I file the surname away for later. "I'm not *homeless*," I say defensively.

Max dips her head and raises her dark eyebrows.

"OK, yes. I'm technically homeless. But, not for long."

"So you keep saying," Max says. She goes to the closet and pulls out a stack of fresh bedsheets.

"You have extra sheets?"

"Yes, I have extra sheets because I'm an adult," Max says, throwing a pillowcase at my face. "Help me."

I drop the dirty sheets and help her wrestle the fitted sheet onto her bed. Her very comfortable bed. "So, spill," Max says.

"Come on, I can't kiss and tell."

Max lifts her nose and sniffs. "You mean fuck and tell, and yes, you can. My bed, remember?"

I grab a pillow and shove it into a pillowcase, catching a faint whiff of Audrey's perfume. Or maybe that's just the laundry detergent. "This smells really good," I say.

"Gain," Max explains.

I make a mental note to buy Gain detergent when I get my own place. I toss the pillow against the headboard. I lift my hands and let them drop. "It was great. Amazing. Like, next level."

"That tells me nothing." Max goes back to the closet.

"You do not have an extra down duvet in there," I say.

Max pulls out a homemade quilt that's seen better days and tosses it on the bed. "No, but you're taking that one to the cleaner's tomorrow."

"OK, OK."

Max goes across the hall to the bathroom. "So, are you going to see her again?"

"Unfortunately, no."

"Toni Danzig has finally found a woman she wants to sleep with more than once?"

"Hey, I don't *only* have one-night stands."

Max gives me The Look.

"OK, yes, I've had a lot of one-night stands. But this didn't feel like one. It was vulnerable. We both were."

"No wham bam thank you ma'am?"

I lean against the bathroom doorjamb as Max brushes her teeth. "Hardly. She's a natural top, that's for sure."

Max nods and says, "Nice" around the toothbrush and foam in her mouth.

"I'm not giving you more details than that."

Max spits and rinses. "No need. I have an imagination."

"I'm going to ignore that comment."

Max shrugs and washes her face.

"What happened after we left Dewey's?"

"Shae left before I could stop her. She didn't come back."

"What do you know about her? Shae?"

"She's some big-shot executive. Sales, I think. The two of them were a bit of a power couple. I've seen them in the Sunday paper a few times, social section for all those business leader bullshit events."

"Oh."

Of course Audrey is out of my league. Even in jeans and a tank she had the put-together aura of a rich, successful woman. Hair that is cut and dyed every six weeks and weekly trips to the dry bar, well-made and expensive clothes, a smooth complexion that is no doubt pampered by an aesthetician on a regular basis, a body that stays fit with a gym membership and a personal trainer. She is so polar opposite of my dirtbag ways we might as well be from different planets. Hey, it's not the first time a rich woman has slummed it with me for a night or two. But the connection with Audrey was... well, it was different. For me, at least.

Max finishes rinsing her face and pats it dry. She hangs the towel and faces me. "Stop it."

"Stop what?"

"Thinking that she's too good for you."

"She's way out of my league."

"Every woman you sleep with is out of your league," Max says, deadpan.

"If you weren't my best friend I'd be offended."

Max shrugs one shoulder. We've known each other all our lives, grew up together. I asked her to be my best friend when I was old enough to put the sentence together. I think we were two. She said yes and here we are, twenty-seven years later. Gentle insults are the norm, with an occasional knock-down drag-out thrown in to clear out our frustrations. Our fights usually end in laughter and we're over it. I get along with Max better than my sister.

"She won't be out of your league come Monday," Max says with a wry smile.

"I am not going to turn into a corporate automaton like my sister."

"She's one of the most respected businesswomen in Colorado. You could do a lot worse."

"You only say that because you've been in love with her since you were twelve."

"Thirteen, but that doesn't change the fact that she's amazing and you could learn a lot from her."

I wave my hand. "Yeah, yeah." I don't want to think about Monday, my first day in the family business.

"How did you leave it?" Max asks. "With Audrey."

"No number. No promises to get together again. She's not in the right place. They just broke up."

"I gathered that from the fuck-you song she sang." Max chuckles. "I would have never imagined she had it in her."

"While she was bringing down the house her sister was at her and Shae's place cleaning it out."

Max's eyebrows lift to her hairline and she laughs. "No shit. I can't decide if that's cowardly or a power move." She flips off the light switch and pushes past me.

Huh. I hadn't thought about it like that. It's a good question.

I turn and follow Max. There's no way I'm going to fall asleep anytime soon.

"Wanna smoke and play *Zelda*?"

"Migraine."

"Shit, Max, you should have told me." Max has suffered from migraines since high school. The best the doctors seem to be able to do is give her medicine to stop it before it starts. It doesn't always work. "Do you need your medicine?"

Max strips down to her boy shorts and sports bra and climbs into bed. "No, I took it when the aura started. I just need a dark room and my bed."

"Let me get you a cold washcloth," I say.

In a couple of minutes I return with the cloth folded in a rectangle. Max has put on an eye mask while I was gone. I sit on the bed and put the washcloth on her forehead.

She gives me a wan smile. "Thanks, Toni."

"You're welcome. Anything else?"

"I'll be fine in the morning."

"Call me if you need me." I lift the washcloth and plant a kiss on her damp forehead.

There's a small smile on her lips and she hums in response.

I pick up the dirty sheets and duvet and close the door softly behind me. The sheets do smell like sex. I smile as I walk into the kitchen to start the laundry. A glance at the oven clock shows it's only been about thirty minutes since Audrey left. Seems longer.

I've wanted to see you like this for a while.

"Oh my God," I mutter, remembering how Audrey's voice caught at the end, how her gaze raked over my body as if she was committing every inch to memory. How my body lit up in response.

That's happening now, too.

"Move. I need to move."

I start the laundry and potter around the kitchen, cleaning

up. Trying my best to not think about Audrey. But how could I not? I've had a lot of good sex with a lot of women, but I've never felt so consumed by someone in my life. I can feel how her hands slid down my body even now, caressing my breasts, trailing lightly over my stomach to my legs, and down to my inner thighs. Her gaze, intense and hungry, on my cunt. The way she took me in her mouth. Her bedroom voice when she said, *Come for me, Toni.*

Christ, it wouldn't take much for me to come right now.

I look around the kitchen and am surprised to find it's spotless. How long have I been daydreaming? I sit at the kitchen table and open my laptop. Email alerts pop up in the top right-hand corner of my screen, one from my sister, no doubt reminding me about being at work bright and early on Monday. I ignore it and open my browser. I click on the search bar, my fingers settle on the keyboard, and I pause.

Audrey Adams. With a name like that how can you not be a successful, high-powered woman. It would take less than a minute to google her and find out everything I want to know. She's a consultant so she's sure to be on LinkedIn and have a website.

I sit back and drop my hands to my lap. What do I want out of this? To see her face? Yes. To find out more about her? Absolutely. To reach out to her? OK, yeah. I do.

But, I can't.

Audrey made it clear that this isn't the right time for her, that she isn't interested in dating. She set a boundary, and finding her on social media and contacting her would cross a line and breach any trust she might have in me. That's not who I am, though my stomach is revolting at the thought of never seeing her again.

I think back to the women who had reached out to me after I made it clear that I wasn't interested in anything more than a night or two of fun. I'd always been nice, or tried to be, except to the ones who would just not leave me alone. I'd always thought they were pathetic and desperate, talking to me about our connection and how they'd never felt that way with someone else. Now here I am, struggling to stop myself from doing the same thing.

Hypocrite, much?

I snap my laptop shut. Nope. Not going to do it. Only three million people live in Denver. I'm sure I'll run into her. Maybe she'll even take me up on my suggestion of role-playing as strangers.

I fall asleep daydreaming about the possibility.

CHAPTER NINE

AUDREY

Willa and I are in the break room of Fourteener Sports, getting coffee to fortify ourselves for our introductory presentation with the company executives. As we're leaving, I'm talking to her over my shoulder and don't see the person walking through the door and straight into me until coffee is splashed all over my white silk shirt.

"Shit," I say, and jump back as if that will save me from the scalding liquid.

Then it's all commotion. The person who ran into me says, "Oh my God I'm so sorry," and the next thing I know they're using their flannel shirt sleeve to wipe off the coffee, which sticks the wet shirt to my skin.

"Thank you, I'm fine," I spit out and immediately regret it. This is our first day as outside consultants for Fourteener Sports and the last thing I need to do is be rude to one of the employees. That's when I look up and see her. Sky-blue eyes. Dark curly hair. Skin that smells like the forest after rain.

Toni.

My one-night stand. The woman who gave me the best night of my life, the woman I haven't stopped thinking about since I walked out her door on weak legs, the woman whose scent I waited until the last possible minute to wash off and have been trying to recreate with my essential oils since, is staring at me in wide-eyed confusion. My eyes go immediately to her arms, which are covered by the aforementioned flannel shirt. Damn it.

Wait. What am I thinking? I can't be ogling at Toni's arms at work.

And hang on just a *fucking* minute. What is Toni doing here?

I dare to meet her eyes and see her staring at Willa, then looking back at me, then back at Willa, who didn't decide to cut her hair into a pixie cut on Saturday, when Toni finally says to my sister, "Audrey?"

And I immediately want to crawl into a hole and die.

"No, I'm Willa Adams. Audrey's sister. We haven't met." She holds out her hand, though Toni is now staring at me.

She hates my hair, I can tell. I decide to do my best to salvage this in the faint hope that Willa won't put two and two together.

"Yes, this is my sister, Willa. Good to see you again, Toni." I hold out my hand.

Toni takes my hand, and I almost jump at the shock that runs up my arm and down to... other parts of my body. The part of my body that's been aching with need all weekend. I never would have thought that you could feel panic and passion simultaneously, but that's exactly what I feel. The last thing I need is for this project, our first project as independent consultants, to go south because I'm distracted by Toni. I'd counted on this project to take Toni off my mind. Yet here she is, looking like a sexy mountain woman and smelling scrumptious and, holy shit, I'm thinking about Friday night and the way she growled, *Audrey, come with me.*

Get a grip, Audrey. You're a professional, and you have a job to do. I try to make my expression neutral. If Toni's furrowed brows and ghost of a smile are any indication, I'm failing miserably. I angle myself away from Willa because she can read me in seconds.

"Nice to see you again, Audrey." Toni then shakes Willa's hand. "I'm Toni Danzig. Nice to meet you...?"

"Willa. Adams. I said before, but you were distracted." She sweeps her hand toward me in an overly grand gesture. "This is Audrey Adams. In case you didn't catch her name."

Shit. Has Willa already figured out Toni was my one-night stand? How does she do that?

"Of course," Toni says. "I didn't know Audrey was an identical twin."

I guess I *had* failed to mention that.

"Besides a regrettably placed tattoo"—Willa shakes her head and sighs—"we're the same."

Toni raises her eyebrows and looks highly amused. She also, very discreetly, gives Willa a once-over.

"I'm the youngest, which means I'm the fun one," Willa says.

"Which means I'm the smart one," I say, giving Willa what I hope is a good imitation of our mother's death stare. Going by the smirk on her face it needs some work. I turn back to Toni. "So, you work here?"

"Yes. Family business, remember?"

"I didn't know *this* was your family business."

How could I have missed that in the research I did on the company when we were creating our pitch for Fourteener Sports' business? There was no mention of Toni at all, though thinking of it now, I realize that there had been two little girls in the grainy photos of the early days at the original store in Aspen.

"I don't tell too many people."

"You'd think my sister was ashamed of us."

Greta Giordani, president and CEO of Fourteener Sports, walks up to our little conclave with a strained smile on her face. She takes in the situation with a glance and her smile turns to something like exasperation, though she tries to hide it.

Sisters? I look between the two women and suppose there's a family resemblance, though you have to look past their two wildly different styles to see it. Toni relaxed, smiling, and a walking advertisement for Fourteener Sports hiking gear, Greta tense and professional in tailored navy trousers and white shirt. The sisters' eyes are arresting, but again in totally different ways. Toni's are a clear, bright blue, while Greta's are a mesmerizing blue with an orange ring around the center. At the moment Greta's eyes are boring into Toni.

"It was an accident," Toni says.

"It always is," Greta says, obviously trying to maintain a professional facade. "Are you OK, Audrey?"

"I'm fine, just..." I pull the shirt away from my chest. "... wet." I glance at Toni and see her mind goes exactly where mine does. Good God, I'm blushing. Willa sees, of course. I know she wants to laugh but she's a professional, thank God, and tries to pull the focus away from me.

"Why don't you tell people you're connected to Fourteener Sports?" Willa says. "This company is amazing. A Colorado legend." She takes Greta in with her comment, who nods and smiles.

"When people find out, they want free stuff." Toni shrugs. "It's just easier."

"Is that why you have a different last name?" Willa asks.

"No, that was just our parents being feminist hippies," Toni says.

"We have a closet full of samples you can take your pick of to replace your shirt, Audrey," Greta says. "Take anything else you like. You too, Willa."

"Free clothes. You're speaking my love language," Willa says.

Greta raises an eyebrow. "You're working in the right place, then."

"So, we're going to be working together," Toni says. She's wearing the same playful expression she had when she mentioned our possible second date.

"Well..." I clear my throat. *Don't look at her lips, don't think about her skin, and whatever you do, don't think about how she spread her legs for you.* Shit. I just thought about it.

"Actually, no," Greta says. "Audrey and Willa's project is focused on operations, not the adventure division. How do you two know each other?"

"Dewey's," Toni says.

"Ah." Greta nods and frowns.

Willa sees it and crosses her arms over her chest. That's never a good sign.

"We should get ready for our presentation," I say. "Excuse us." I narrow my eyes at Toni. I didn't necessarily want to be outed at work. My sexuality isn't a secret, and I'm not ashamed of it, but it's not something I talk about either.

Toni seems to realize what she's done and now it's her turn to blush.

I push through the group and am walking down the hall before Toni can reply. I hear Willa say something to her, which makes her laugh, and mother ducker if a big green lightning bolt of jealousy doesn't hit me right in the stomach. I refuse to look back, though I want to. Desperately.

I plop into my desk chair. Of course the sexy one-night stand who I've been trying to forget about for the last fifty-two hours and fifteen minutes is here, looking good enough to eat in her plaid sky-blue flannel and fleece vest, her dark hair in a side braid that lies across her breast just so, hair that looked incredibly wild and free and hot when I unbraided and ran my hands through it on Friday night.

I turn away and pretend that she isn't chatting amiably with Willa, my identical twin, and walking right toward me, Greta one step behind. My phone buzzes. I don't recognize the number, but I recognize the message. Shae has taken to texting me from random numbers since I blocked hers on Friday night. I'm regretting waving a red flag in front of Shae like I did. I put my phone in airplane mode and lay it face down on the desk.

"Let's get you a new shirt," Greta says.

"I'll take care of it," Toni says. "I'm sure you have some big important CEO thing to do."

Greta narrows her eyes at Toni and glances between the two of us. She looks at her watch. "The meeting starts in ten minutes, Toni." Greta turns and leaves and Toni salutes her. I hear someone in the open concept office chuckle.

Toni is grinning when she turns to me, but her smile slides off her face when she sees my expression. "Just sister stuff," she says. "You have a twin. You get it."

"I think Willa and I have a very different relationship than you and Greta," I say.

"The whole twin thing," Toni says.

"No. Mutual respect," I reply.

Toni's mouth drops open a bit, then closes. Her shoulders slump.

Willa grabs my computer bag from my desk and says, "And, on that note, I'll go get everything set up."

"That wasn't very professional of me, I guess," Toni says.

"No, especially not in front of the employees." I glance around the open office. Though the cubicles are divided by low walls, there's no privacy and everyone nearby heard Toni's lack of respect for Greta.

"Right. Sorry. For that and before. I shouldn't have mentioned..."

I clear my throat and look around pointedly.

"Oh, right," Toni says. "Come with me." She gently grabs my hand and turns me around to follow her before dropping it.

Professionalism, Audrey. Put aside the fact that the last time this woman led you down a hall you had three incredibly satisfying orgasms and gave her four. It doesn't matter that you had the best sex of your life with this woman, that she was the first woman you've come with simultaneously, that the intense emotions from Friday night continue to linger deep in your chest. Focus on the slight sway of her hips in those very, very, well-fitting hiking pants. No, Audrey. Focus on the meeting you have in ten minutes.

"Audrey?"

I jerk my head up and realize she's busted me checking out her ass. Well, there's only one thing to do, brazen it out and change the subject.

"You undersold your family business on Friday."

"Yes, well. Like I said, I get tired of people wanting freebies. But I'll make an exception for you." She opens a metal door and waves me into a long narrow room with floor-to-ceiling shelves full of what looks to be one of every piece of clothing in their catalog. Toni turns to me, her shoulders hunched, and puts her hands in her front pockets. "I'm sorry I mentioned Dewey's like that," Toni says. "I realize I might have just outed you. Not that everyone who goes to Dewey's is gay, but yeah. I shouldn't have done that. Greta doesn't care, obviously." She waves her hands at herself. "Big dyke for a sister, and all."

"Actually, it wasn't *obvious*."

"Greta's always had resting bitch face, trust me."

I narrow my eyes at her again.

"Right, sorry. Unprofessional. It's something I need to work on, I know."

Toni looks truly abashed, which is a relief. Her behavior for the last five minutes has made me realize how little I know about her. Her ability to see her mistakes, admit them, and apologize is refreshing. And, dammit, it's attractive. It would be easier for my professionalism, and my willpower, if she would continue to act like an immature little sister. Because, Jesus, we're going to have to work together. Or in the same building, at least.

"Thank you for apologizing," I say.

Toni smiles, looking relieved. She rolls up the sleeves of her shirt.

Look up, Audrey. Look up. Stop drooling over her forearms. You're a professional and at work, for Chrissake. When I meet Toni's gaze she's grinning.

"You did that on purpose," I say.

"Did what?"

I wiggle my finger in the vicinity of her forearms. "You know what you did."

She crosses her arms and flexes them. I can't help but laugh, and Toni laughs with me.

She waves a hand at the clothes. "Pick what you want."

"Oh, I couldn't."

"I ruined your shirt, which I'll replace. You heard Greta. Take what you like."

"How much older is Greta than you?"

"Three years. She never lets me live it down, just like you lord it over Willa."

I roll my eyes. Of course, that would be one of the first things Willa tells Toni. "More like Willa uses being younger as an excuse for everything."

"Sounds like my kinda woman."

"My sister is a flirt, but she's straight." What the hell? Why did I say that?

Toni leans against a shelf and raises her eyebrow, the mannerism identical to Greta's. "Is she? Interesting."

"What?"

"I was getting a bi vibe. Or maybe she was checking me out to make sure I'm good enough for you."

"She doesn't know you were the one."

"The one?" Toni's eyes sparkle with mischief.

"My one-night stand."

"Oh, you told her about us?"

"Not technically, no." When Toni waits for me to continue, I say, "It was a little obvious when I didn't get home until after two in the morning. Apparently I don't have a poker face."

She breaks into a gorgeous big grin. Dammit. Stop being so beautiful and endearing and fucking sexy in hiking clothes, of all things. I've never, in my entire time living in Colorado, been attracted to the sporty outdoorsy lesbians, which, let's be honest, means I have a drastically shallow dating pool. But if Toni offered to take me into the backcountry and build me a cabin and live off the grid, I might just throw everything away and go.

"Hello?" Toni waves her hand in front of my eyes. "Where'd you go there? Or should I ask?"

I clear my throat. "Probably better not to."

Toni grins, but thankfully doesn't ask for details. "Do you want me to pick something for you? You know what? I will."

She is in my personal space now, trying to squeeze between me and the shelf. I could shift back to let her through, but my body won't move.

"I can pick out my own clothes," I say, though I can barely hear my voice.

"I know." Her gaze moves to my hair. "I like your new haircut."

"You didn't recognize me."

"In my defense, it's a pretty drastic change. I loved your long hair, but this..." She lets out a low whistle.

"You're just saying that."

"No, I'm really not. It suits you."

"It makes me look like a giraffe."

"That's not what I think of when I look at your neck."

I should probably say my stomach flip-flops or something like that, but that is definitely not where I feel that comment.

"I think you know what your neck makes me think of," Toni says.

I want her to move closer, but she stays still. No. No I don't want her to move closer. I'm at work. This is an important contract; I need to be clear-headed. Then I realize *I* could be the one who moves away, so I start looking at the items on the shelves.

"Um, no, we, um should talk about working together. Boundaries," I say.

"Like Greta said, we won't be working together. I'm running the adventure division. I have nothing to do with manufacturing or shipping or any of that other super boring stuff you talked about the other night. Absolutely no conflict of interest."

With enough space between us I turn to Toni again.

"Everything I said the other night still holds true. I had a great time with you, but I'm getting out of a toxic relationship. I need time and space."

"And as I said the other night, I totally get it."

"Even if that wasn't an obstacle, we would have to put this on hold for this project. It's our first project on our own and the last thing Willa and I need is to do anything that would undermine our professional reputation and—"

"Audrey, I get it."

"I wasn't finished," I say.

Toni's eyes widen at the snappiness in my voice. I don't apologize. I really don't like being interrupted.

"At my last job, I blew the whistle on an inappropriate affair between an executive and one of his subordinates. I wasn't fired, but I was passed over for a promotion I deserved because of it.

That's why I'm an independent consultant. I've never had an inappropriate work relationship, and I'm not about to start now." *No matter how much I want to kiss those lips of hers*, I think.

Toni nods. "I won't lie and say I'm not disappointed, because I am. I had a great time the other night and really want to get to know you better."

I open my mouth to respond but Toni holds up her hand.

"I'm not finished," she says, with a wink and grin. I chuckle and nod. "I'm not going to do anything that would jeopardize your business or this project. It's important to Greta, and the company. But I do have to warn you..."

I raise my eyebrows.

"I've been told I'm pretty fucking charming, so you'll have to be strong." She shrugs her shoulders as if she's helpless against her nature.

I roll my eyes. "Oh my God you are so much like my sister. I'm pretty sure I can resist you. I imagine you'll be out guiding most of the time."

"I may fill in for a guide here and there in our desert hikes, but it's off season here in Colorado. I'll be working regular office hours, though I have a couple of overseas hikes planned for January and February."

"Oh." I don't hate the idea of Toni being around. It will be nice to get to know her a bit better. I suppose "better" is an interesting word choice here. It will be nice to get to know Toni on a professional level, maybe even as friends. The challenge will be keeping my mind on business when she's just so goddamn nice to look at with those eyes and that amused smile on her face—

Aaaaand I'm staring at her. I clear my throat and turn away. I reach for a Fourteener blue puffy vest then pull my hand back. It's their bestseller and it costs a pretty penny. I should go for something more reasonable. I see a white button-down tech shirt that will be an OK substitute for the day.

"Here," Toni says.

I turn around with the shirt and she's holding up the vest. "Consider it the first part of my repayment for ruining your shirt."

I want it, I've always wanted one, but I hate being given it. I like to earn my splurges.

Toni shakes the vest. "You're going to be late for our meeting. Here." She shoves the vest in my arms. "Change into the shirt and vest. I'll wait outside."

She leaves and I change. I put my arms through the vest, zip it up, and put my hands in the pockets. It's a perfect fit.

I step outside and Toni's eyes light up. "Looks great on you. Though I'm guessing you're the type of woman who looks great in everything."

"Thank you. For the vest and shirt."

"You're welcome. Friends?" She holds out her hand.

I take it and feel the shock. The way Toni's eyes narrow slightly, she feels it too.

"Friends," I say.

Toni smiles and nods. "Now, let's go see if I can stay awake during your presentation." She winks at me, and my insides go all gooey and soft.

So much for being strong.

CHAPTER TEN

TONI

I have no idea what Audrey and Willa's presentation is about. I'm sure it is excellent; the department heads around the table ask questions and everyone seems pleased with the answers. All I can focus on is watching Audrey and thinking I'm the luckiest dirtbag in the world. When she walked out early Saturday morning, I didn't think I'd ever see her again yet here she is, starting a months-long project at my family's company, somehow even sexier and more beautiful in buttoned-up business expert mode than she was in sexy scorned lover mode.

I think I'm in love.

Tamp it down, Danzig. Audrey has set professional boundaries, and you are going to respect them. Outwardly. Inwardly, I can pine and long and admit that these are going to be the most excruciating six months, or more, of my life.

Greta says something in her irritated bossy voice, and I tear my gaze away from Audrey. Yep, Greta is staring at me and is not amused. And everyone else is staring at me with expectant expressions. Audrey is looking down at her notes, her cheeks pink. Willa looks like her birthday came early.

"I'm sorry, what?" I say to Greta.

Her narrowed eyes tell me I'm going to hear about this later. "Welcome back," she says, and I'm not sure if she means from the field or from my daydream.

"Thanks. It's great to finally be in the office."

Everyone around the table laughs. My disdain for office work and all business bureaucracy is well known. Audrey purses her lips and looks disapproving.

"Yeah, yeah," I say, laughing with them. "I mean it. By this time next year, the adventure division will be the fastest growing adventure company in the United States."

Greta waves her hand at me. "Great. Let's hear it."

"Hear what?"

"Your plan." She crosses her arms. She's tapping her foot impatiently. I can't see it, but I can tell.

"Um, well..."

My mind goes completely blank. What are my plans? I have them. I've been thinking about them for months. I've got dozens of voice memos on my phone with ideas I had while leading tours but not one of them will come to mind. Audrey's watching me, and when I catch her eye, she smiles and nods in encouragement. Warmth surges through me. At least someone is on my side.

"I have lots of voice notes, I just haven't put them all together yet. It's number one on my to-do list for the week. I'll have it for you next Monday. But don't expect a PowerPoint presentation like the professionals gave."

"I'm sure whatever you put together will be wonderful, Goat," Ned Stevens, our head of manufacturing says.

"Goat?" Willa says. "As in Greatest of All Time?"

"No," I interject before Ned can say anything. "It's a childhood nickname that turned into my trail name."

"She's always been like a billy goat on the trails," Ned says. "There was this one time—"

"No stories, Ned," I say. "This is where you end the meeting, Greta."

I can tell she's thinking about doing some good-natured teasing of her own, and I'm ready for it. I live for sparring with my sister. But Greta's professionalism wins out, as usual.

"Now, for the most important item on our agenda," Greta says, "the holiday party!"

All the department heads cheer as the HR director talks about plans for the company party for all employees and family members in three weeks' time. It's the highlight of everyone's year, including mine. Nothing makes me happier than dressing up like Buddy the Elf and helping Ned as Kris Kringle hand out presents to the employees' kids, and seeing the looks on the employees' and their partners' faces when they get to take their pick of the new clothing items for their own holiday present.

Once all the details are discussed, and Audrey and Willa are invited and accept, the meeting is adjourned. Greta pulls Audrey aside and they are immediately in deep conversation.

"Great presentation," I say to Willa, keeping one eye on Audrey.

Willa scoffs. "You didn't hear a word we said."

"That obvious?"

"Yeah. I was shocked Audrey didn't spontaneously combust from your laser-like focus, but that's Audrey for you. All business."

"Yeah," I say, watching Greta and Audrey. Both remarkably alike in their all-business demeanors. I've always found it off-putting in Greta, but damn if it isn't a bit of a turn-on when I switch my gaze to Audrey. That's going to take some unpacking with my therapist, i.e. Max, tonight over a beer.

Willa finishes packing her computer. "So how do you and Audrey know each other?"

The question sounds innocent enough. Too innocent. I'm determined not to say anything that would give me the pursed lips and disapproving stare from Audrey again.

"We met Friday night at the Dew Drop Inn. She got on stage and sang a fuck-you break-up song to her ex. Brought the house down."

"She *what*?"

Greta and Audrey join us. "Toni, Audrey is going to help you pull together your business plan this week."

I could kiss my sister right now. "Great," I say in as professional a voice as I can muster.

"Gather whatever you need and meet me back here once you're done meeting with Greta," Audrey says.

I can't tell if she's happy about this change in her project timeline or not.

"Sounds good." I know I have a goofy grin on my face, but I mean, seriously? Spending the next week working one on one with Audrey is a freaking gift. I might just have to kiss my sister. Instead, I follow her down the hall to her office. She tells me to shut the door and drops her iPad on the desk a little harder than she probably should.

"What the hell, Toni?"

"What do you mean?"

"I would say I can't believe you came to the meeting with nothing prepared, but this is you we're talking about."

"Hey. Just a minute. I've been out in the field. I haven't had time to sit at a computer for hours putting together some stupid presentation to go over all the ideas I've been telling you about for months."

"Oh, really? What did you do this weekend?"

"Had fun. It was the holidays. Thanksgiving? Remember the big-ass turkey we ate with Mom and Dad? Let me guess, you worked all weekend."

"It was Black Friday; of course I worked. And a good thing. Our servers crashed with all the traffic."

"Our business was just fine before you decided we needed to compete with—"

Greta holds up a perfectly manicured hand that hasn't clutched a rock face in at least a decade. "I'm not going to have this argument with you again. Besides, didn't you just say we would have the biggest adventure business in America in a year? You're as ambitious as I am, you just have your whole"— she waves her hand—"devil-may-care mountain woman aesthetic to maintain."

I open my mouth to respond but clamp it shut instead. There is no point in fighting with Greta. Our personalities are night and day. She's all structure and rules and I'm a hippie dirtbag who knows nature laughs at structure and rules and can adapt to unexpected situations on a moment's notice. Greta keeps me in line, and I keep her from taking herself too seriously all the time. Or at least we try. We fail more often than not, though.

"Why were you staring at Audrey like a kid with a Christmas puppy?" Greta asks.

"I wasn't."

Greta scoffs. "You've slept with her before, haven't you?"

"No."

Greta sighs and sits down, and motions for me to do the same. "When?" she asks.

"When what?"

Greta gives me the big sister *stop with the bullshit* expression.

"Friday night," I confess.

"As in two days ago?"

"More like sixty hours, but yeah."

Greta puts her head in her hands.

"I had no idea who she was, and she didn't know who I was," I say.

My sister sighs and shakes her head. "You live in a whole other world than I do."

"Yes, I get laid regularly and you don't."

"I don't want to just *get laid*, Antonia."

"No need to pull out the full name, *Gertrude*."

"Not my name," Greta singsongs. She flips open her iPad and taps on the keyboard. "Is this going to be a problem? Working with her? You didn't ghost her, did you?"

"No, of course not."

"Were you planning on seeing each other again?"

"Not exactly. But not because anything bad happened. The opposite, if you want to know the truth."

"I actually *don't* want to know about your sex life. It's bad enough I'm going to have a visual of you two every time I see you together."

"Look at you, straight girl, having lesbian fantasies. Though keep me out of them, please. That's a little creepy, Gertie."

"Oh my God. I've changed my mind. You're better suited to be in the field, not the office. Feel free to move your trip to New Zealand up to tomorrow. Or tonight would be even better."

"Ha. Wild horses couldn't drag me out of here now."

Greta narrows her eyes. "Seriously, Toni. Your relationship with Audrey Adams needs to be just business while they're working with us. Once the project is done, you can have as many spectacular nights with her as you want." She puts on her reading glasses, which is her non-verbal way of dismissing people.

"For the record, Audrey and I have already talked about it."

Greta looks up in surprise.

"Boundaries have been agreed to. Professionalism promised, on both sides," I continue.

"I'm not worried about Audrey. Do *not* let your libido interfere with her job."

"I thought *I* was her job."

"Only for a week. Now go, get to work. I want to be wowed next Monday."

CHAPTER ELEVEN

AUDREY

"It's Toni, isn't it? Your one-night stand," Willa stage-whispers as we walk out of the conference room.

There is no point in denying it to Willa, of all people, but I don't have to confirm it, either.

"And what's this I hear about you singing *karaoke* that night?" Willa says.

"You told me to make sure Shae stayed away."

"You said you were just going to watch that she didn't leave the bar, not go in and tell her to fuck off from the stage. I am so *proud* of you. Oh my gosh. I wish I'd been there to see the look on that douche canoe's face."

I grinned. "It was pretty epic."

"Goddamn right you were," Willa says.

"I don't know what came over me."

"Whatever it was, tap into it more often. Especially if you're tapping into Toni Danzig."

"Willa."

"Finally, you're interested in someone I approve of."

"You barely know her."

"She's much better for you than Shae."

I stop abruptly. "How in the world could you decide that on two minutes of conversation?" I hold up my hand. "And don't give me that gift of discernment bullshit."

Willa grins. "I might not know Toni, but I know Shae and she was wrong for you from the start." I glare at her. "You're right. I'm sorry. Let's talk about Toni instead."

"Willa, there's nothing to talk about. We had a one-night stand. Now we work together. I've explained to her why nothing at all can happen between us and she gets it. So, no playing matchmaker."

"Me? I would never. You're right. No hanky-panky while we're on this project. But after..."

"Oh, hey, look," I say. "Here comes Kris Kringle to get you out of my hair."

Willa waves at Ned and says, "Give me two minutes."

"Meet you in the lobby." He hitches his pants up over his dad belly and ambles through the office, smiling and waving at everyone along the way.

"He really is a perfect Santa Claus," I say. I wish I was working with Ned. No distraction there at all.

"Truer words have never been spoken," Willa replies.

My phone buzzes again, like it has dozens of times since Saturday night. I regret my decision each time it does. I should have known that she would double down on her efforts to convince me to come back, not rethink her shitty behavior. Note to self: never publicly humiliate someone with narcissistic personality disorder. Or a Pisces.

"Shae with a new number?" Willa asks.

"Yes." I block the number and delete the message.

"Hey." Willa puts her hands on my shoulders and turns me to face her. "Take a deep breath." I do it because it's easier than arguing. "Do you want me to talk to Shae?"

"No. I want to ignore her and pretend she doesn't exist."

"That's probably not the right direction to take with her, but OK."

"She'll give up eventually."

Willa nods but doesn't look convinced.

"Now," Willa says, "about Toni. I really do like her, and you can't ever have too many friends. As long as I'm always number one, of course."

"Naturally."

"Promise me you won't be all business."

"But this is—"

Willa puts her fingers on my lips to silence me. "I'm not saying bend her over the conference table and show her who's boss, just relax and be yourself. Don't be gruff business Audrey." She removes her fingers.

"Can I talk now?" I ask.

Willa nods.

"I am going to be a professional hired to do a job. I set personal boundaries on Saturday and professional boundaries this morning. Toni will respect them. If she doesn't, then that will be that."

"Exactly. But what if *you* don't respect them?" Willa asks.

I narrow my eyes at her.

"Right. This is you we're talking about."

"Ned's waiting," I say. "Have fun at the warehouse. See you tonight." I lightly punch her in the shoulder for a goodbye, which is just as awkward as it sounds.

Willa laughs, rolls her eyes, and calls me a dork.

I'm grinning when I walk into the conference room—Willa's laugh has always done that to me—and stop cold in the doorway. There's Toni, leaning across the conference table to grab a pen, her hiking pants hugging her ass on full display. My mind immediately goes exactly where Willa meant for it to. I'm going to *kill* her.

"You OK?" Toni says.

I shake my head and smile. "Yes. Perfect." I sit down in front of my computer and wake it. "Why don't you tell me about your plans, and I'll take notes."

"Great. Yeah." Toni pulls out her phone and opens the voice app.

"Wait." I place my hand over hers and goosebumps race up my arm. I can't move my hand; it's as if some magnetic force has forged us together. We stare at our hands for a few seconds, or maybe longer, I honestly have no idea, before our gazes meet. I know I should say something, but what? My mind fills with the memory of gripping Toni's hands while I went down on her, her grip painful when she shuddered to her third climax. I flush with desire from head to toe which means I look like I'm breaking out into hives.

I remove my hand from hers. "Let's—" I clear the huskiness out of my throat. I want to fan myself but resist the urge. Maybe Toni hasn't noticed my blotching. "Just talk it out."

"Sure. Yeah. OK." Toni's voice is strained and a little high-pitched, like a teenager's. "What was the question?" I feel a smile tug at the corners of my mouth and Toni laughs. "So much for being professional. Sorry. I just, um... you felt that too, right?"

I nod. "I felt it, too."

Toni sighs, but she's grinning. "Thank God."

Now I'm laughing. "What was that sigh for?"

"Well, I'd prepared myself for the typical rom-com story-line. We pretend to be professional, have a stupid misunderstanding that normal people wouldn't have because they have basic communication skills."

I laugh again. "In my experience very few people have basic communication skills, especially when it comes to relationships."

"But we're not like that, you see. Here we are, supposed to

be working but we're talking about stupid rom-com tropes. This wouldn't happen until the mid-point of the story and here it is, happening in the first act."

"Are you sure we're still in the first act?" I tease, playing along with Toni's analogy.

"Hmm. Good point. Maybe we are at the mid-point."

"Are you a writer?"

"God, no. Sitting in front of a computer for hours all alone trying to put my thoughts into words and then down on paper? That's my seventh circle of hell. But"—she raises her finger—"I took a screenwriting class in college because the teacher was hot. She taught me a lot. Even a little bit about story structure."

Toni looks so cute and mischievous and I can't help but wonder how I benefited from her "screenwriting" education. I shift in my chair and cross my legs. Toni notices, but doesn't say anything.

My computer dings and dings and dings. Leave it to Shae to dump cold water on my good mood. Willa is right. I'm going to have to talk to her eventually because she is obviously not going to give up. I've already blocked five numbers and she isn't taking the hint. I mute my computer as quickly as possible but Toni can see the screen.

"You're popular," she teases.

"I'd rather not be. It's Shae."

"Is she bothering you?"

"Yes, but I shouldn't have humiliated her in public. I think she wants me back so she can publicly dump me."

Toni studies me with a worried expression. "You shouldn't blame yourself because Shae won't leave you alone."

"I'm not."

Toni's expression doesn't change.

"Did I?"

"A little, yeah. Why haven't you blocked her?"

"I have. She keeps texting me from different numbers."

"So, she's stalking you."

I inhale, exhale, and give my best professional smile. "Let's talk business. Tell me your plans," I say.

Toni nods. "OK. My plan is for Fourteener Trekking to expand into corporate team-building tours and leverage the money we make from them to fund hiking programs for marginalized kids and adults."

"Stop right there," I say, and write down what she said. "That's a perfect elevator pitch."

"I don't know what that is."

She is so cute and guileless I want to grab her cheeks and kiss her. I don't of course. Maybe Willa had a point about me not respecting my own boundaries. I shake the thought out of my head and return my focus to Toni's pitch.

"Imagine you're trying to sell me on this idea and all the time you have is a short elevator ride. A couple of sentences to summarize your product or idea. That's an elevator pitch. Go on."

"I want to create an outdoor education curriculum and lobby states to include it in their school curriculum. I want to expand our women-only tours and be a safe space for trans men and women to experience nature. I also want to expand outside of the US and partner with local, experienced guides around the world. My initial focus is on South America. So much wilderness to explore. Of course, we would only partner with tour operators who are focused on conservation, which might raise the cost a bit, but corporate accounts won't mind and, as a rule, people who take outdoor adventure vacations are eco conscious. We could do eco tours that include volunteering for a day or two, as well.

"Part of me hates focusing on corporate business clients. But they're willing and able to pay. We will take those profits and put as much as we can toward our real mission: making sure everyone, no matter what their situation, has a chance to get out into nature."

"You can also leverage those corporate relationships into a source of donations for your foundation. I'm assuming you want to set up a non-profit foundation for your charity work?" I say, typing as fast as I can.

"Um, I guess so. I hadn't gotten that far."

I smile. "That's why I'm here. A curriculum is an excellent idea, but education budgets are being cut all over the country. You'll probably have to fund those programs through your foundation, which means corporate support."

"Riiight."

"What's wrong?" I ask.

She gives me a small smile. "It sounded so simple in my mind. Now it sounds really hard and complex."

I remove my hands from my keyboard. "We're brainstorming, Toni. That means pie in the sky ideas. From what little you've said, this project will need to be broken down into stages. It will probably take five years for you to get half of what you want, and ten years to get the rest, and even then, you won't get everything you've mentioned. It seems daunting, I'm sure, but everything you've said is doable. We just have to be methodical in how we go about it. So, dream big right now, OK? We have all week to turn your ideas into an action plan. Or a rough outline of one. Action plans change each year, too, based on what was achieved and not achieved the year before."

"Oh man, I'm really not cut out for corporate work," Toni says.

"That all sounded awful to you, didn't it?"

"A little, yeah."

"Tell you what, let's think of this as if we are going to hire someone else to implement it. You'll still be in the field, trekking all day every day."

Toni smiles. "Sounds like a plan. Which reminds me,

Friday night you promised to go on a hike with me. How does Sunday sound?"

I laugh. "I promised no such thing."

"Huh, I could have sworn you did." Toni's grinning. "Anyway, it would be a good idea for you to experience a guided hike. It would be research for this project. Helping me."

"I don't need to go on a hike to help you create a business plan, Toni. Besides, this weekend you will be practicing your presentation so you can blow Greta's socks off on Monday."

"Working on a Sunday?"

"You guide on Sundays, don't you?"

"Yeah, but that doesn't feel like work."

"So, you're saying spending time with me will feel like work?" I tease.

"Spending time with you is the only saving grace to all this work, let me tell you."

"Come on, you can't tell me that proving Greta wrong about you isn't a big motivation."

"Well, that, too." Her smile drops a bit. "Um, somehow, Greta realized we'd, you know, and told me to keep it professional."

"She knows?" Christ. "How did she figure that out?"

"Apparently I was looking at you like you were a Christmas puppy."

I laugh. Greta Giordani obviously has a dry wit Willa and I haven't seen yet.

Toni chuckles, but she's a little red in the face. "Was I?"

"Maybe a little."

Toni furrows her brows and taps her chin with her finger. "And how did that make you feel?" she says in a breathy, thoughtful voice.

I laugh. I haven't laughed so much with another woman, besides Willa, in years. "You sound exactly like my therapist."

Our gazes lock. There is so much electricity between us I'm surprised literal sparks aren't flying through the air.

"How about we table that question and answer for a few weeks, huh?"

"Only a few weeks?"

"OK, Casanova. Stop. Let's get to work making your dream a reality."

CHAPTER TWELVE

AUDREY

The whine of the vacuum cleaner stops and the air fills with the faint sound of Christmas music. Willa pulls the cord out of the wall and winds it around the hooks on the handle. "Let's invite Toni and Greta over for dinner, she said. It'll be fun, she said."

I roll my eyes. Vacuuming the house is Willa's favorite chore, though God knows why.

"I saw that," she says.

"You had your back to me."

"Your eye rolls are deafening."

"Your protests are lame," I say. "We've barely been here all week. You didn't need to vacuum."

Willa puts a hand on her hip. "We can't have Greta and Toni come over and the place be a mess."

I pause, very briefly, in stirring the roux for my seafood gumbo. We've only been in our townhome for a week, but it looks amazing. We decorated for Christmas on Sunday. The tree is standing by the front bay window, its multicolored lights glowing pleasantly through to the street.

"You're right," Willa says. "The place looks great." She puts the vacuum up, fluffs some pillows because she really can't help herself, and finally pours us two glasses of Sauvignon Blanc. She pushes one across the kitchen island and sits on a barstool. "So, is there some sort of code word, or a gesture or something when you want me to execute the plan?" she asks.

The plan came to me on Friday afternoon, when Toni was trying and failing for the fourth time to practice her presentation. All week while we worked together, I'd watched Toni's confidence wax and wane, going from self-assured and confident, bordering on cockiness, to being humbled at the scope of her idea and the amount of work it would take. A couple of times I thought she might give up, but a well-timed check-in from Greta on Wednesday had been enough to motivate her. I'm still not sure if Toni wants to make Greta proud or prove her wrong. I suspect it's a bit of both. You better believe I subtly pushed those buttons every time I saw her attention start to wane.

By Friday the presentation was ready, and Toni stood at the front of the conference room and fidgeted from foot to foot, looking ill at ease and struggling to put a coherent sentence together. She was a little better each time, but something would trip her up and she would go back to the beginning to start over. When I saw sweat run down her temple, I knew that as confident as Toni is in other areas of her life, public speaking isn't one of them.

After a week of working with Toni, soaking in her enthusiasm, and marveling at her knowledge, I was as invested in her vision for the adventure division, and as sure of its success, as she was. Failure wasn't an option, so I needed to get creative. I invited the sisters over for dinner under the guise of us all getting to know each other better. The invitation caught Willa as off guard as it did Greta and Toni, since she's usually the one offering invitations and planning our social life. But she was onboard immediately, and when I told her the reason her enthusiasm only grew.

"Nothing so clandestine," I say. "Just ask Toni about her ideas. Make it seem natural."

"She'll be pitching to Greta without realizing it," Willa says, taking a healthy sip of her wine. She sighs contentedly. "You have amazing taste in wine."

"Exactly, and thank you. Toni will never admit it, but she's terrified of letting Greta down."

Willa nods. "I'm sure it's difficult being in Greta's shadow. She's successful, smart, well-respected, and a leader in her field."

"I thought you didn't like Greta."

"Oh, I respect her professionally, but I wouldn't want to hang out with her. I can only handle one uptight, perfectionist woman in my life and that's you."

"Um, thanks?"

"You're welcome." Willa sets down her glass and leans forward. "Greta and Toni don't have a relationship like ours. And it has nothing to do with us being twins."

Now it's my turn to raise an eyebrow at Willa.

"OK, maybe a little. Your idea is great, but don't expect them to leave here tonight singing 'Kumbaya' and communicating with their eyebrows."

"Eyebrows are *our* secret code."

"Damn right it is, and we share it with no one."

"I don't think either one wants to give the other credit for what they've achieved," I say.

"From what I've heard," Willa says, "Toni's been trying to keep up with her big sister since she was old enough to walk, and Greta has some pretty big footsteps to fill."

"Yeah, I got that impression when we were talking Friday night."

"You *talked* Friday night?"

"Fuck off, Willa," I say, but I'm laughing.

Against all odds, Willa and I have never been competitive. From a young age we carved out our own niches and never felt the urge to one-up each other. We both made good grades, got into University of Texas with full rides, and we are both very good at our jobs. There is very little inequality in our relationship, and where there is a weakness it's in an area the other is strong. We manage to balance each other perfectly. I suspect Toni and Greta would, too, if they'd just meet halfway.

I confess that I've done some research on Toni since Monday when we literally ran into each other, which basically means stalking her on Instagram and TikTok. My palms get sweaty merely thinking about some of the daredevil, harebrained things she's done, and there is plenty of video proof of each one. How she hasn't broken every bone in her body is a minor miracle. She has 25,000 followers on Instagram, and a majority of those seem to be fangirls who flirt shamelessly with her in the comments section of her posts. That doesn't make me jealous. At all.

It's not that I can blame them. Toni might do things that I think are insane and I would never do to save my life, but she's not foolhardy about it. Before every stunt she pulls, she goes into detail about the safety precautions she's taking, the training she's done, the experience she has, and gives out resources for others to use if they want to train for something similar, before ending with a stern admonishment to absolutely not try this at home without preparation or a professional nearby. Toni's athleticism and skill are hot, but it is her expertise and intelligence that lit a fire inside me late at night while watching her videos, a fire that lingered during the day while working side by side.

It's time to put this Toni project to bed so I can move on to what I was hired to do, and to also put some well-needed personal distance between us. My attraction to her is taking up way too much space in my head, and my body.

"I get the impression that Toni has been indulged by her parents," Willa says to break my wandering thoughts.

I raise my eyebrows.

"Ned likes to talk."

I am about to ask Willa to elaborate when the doorbell rings.

CHAPTER THIRTEEN

TONI

Greta and I might be as different as night and day, but one thing we have in common is punctuality. Dad hammered "On time is ten minutes early" into our brains at a very young age. Which is how we both end up approaching Willa and Audrey's front door at exactly seven twenty.

"Wine and a plant? Isn't that a bit overboard?" I ask.

"Wine is for dinner. The plant is a housewarming gift."

"Oh," I say. I'm holding two six-packs of craft beer and suddenly feel like I'm failing at being an adult.

"It can be from both of us," Greta says, pushing the doorbell.

"Oh, thanks. Let me know how much I owe you."

Greta gives me a look. "Don't be silly. You look really cute."

I glance down. For the first time in as long as I can remember I'm not wearing Fourteener gear. Jeans, a cream-colored fisherman's sweater I stole from my dad a few years ago, my favorite pair of Onitsuka Tigers, a thrifted olive-green pea coat, and my hair is down and wild, like Audrey likes it. I'd sent a selfie to Max asking if I looked like I was trying too hard.

LOL. No.

"Max said I look like I'm about to haul in my lobster pots," I say.

Greta's eyes widen, she looks me up and down, and busts out laughing. I grin. Greta has a great laugh; it's deep and throaty, as if it's come from the very depths of her soul. I don't even mind being on the receiving end. I miss hearing it.

"She's not wrong," Greta says.

The door opens and Willa greets us with a smile on her face and a glass of white wine in her hand. She's wearing faded, slouchy boyfriend jeans and a long navy cashmere cardigan over a white T-shirt. Her hair is up in a messy bun and she is either not wearing makeup or has mastered the natural makeup look. Her look is so casually effortless it must have taken a lot of work.

"Bang on time. Come in, come in," she says and steps aside.

"We're a little early," Greta says.

"Early is on time. Come in," Willa says.

"No wonder you hired them," I murmur to Greta as we enter. "Oh my God something smells amazing," I then say.

Audrey walks up, a kitchen towel thrown over her shoulder, a warm and welcoming smile on her face. "We're glad y'all could make it," she says.

Audrey looks great, which is no surprise. Her short hair is very carefully mussed, unlike the sleek style she wears at work. She wears black tights, a roomy untucked light-blue button-down shirt, and bright red lipstick on her very, very kissable lips.

"This is from both of us." Greta holds the plant out to Willa.

"A money plant. I like how you think," Willa says.

"I thought I'd get a succulent since I wasn't sure if you were plant people. I figured between the two of you one would remember to water it." Greta glances around the room where plants of all sizes, shapes, and colors give it a cozy, lived-in feeling. "I needn't have worried."

"That's all Willa," Audrey says. "In fact, she has all the style."

Willa holds her hands out in an exaggerated shrug. "Guilty as charged. Audrey is the food and wine connoisseur."

Audrey makes the same gesture and reaches for the wine Greta holds out. "Thank you."

I hold up the beer. "I guess I'll drink this by myself."

"Not on your life," Willa says.

"Something smells delicious," Greta says. She sheds her coat and reaches out for mine.

"Seafood gumbo," Audrey says.

"Here, give me those," Willa says. She reaches for the coats, but Greta says to point her in the right direction. Willa leads her out of the room. We watch them leave and don't look at each other until we hear their chatter almost completely fade.

When I turn, I catch Audrey's gaze traveling up my body.

"Hi," I say, my own gaze drawn to her bright red lips.

"Hi, yourself. You look..." Her eyes travel down again, and she licks her lips. "Um, very nice."

Lobsterman, my ass.

"So do you." I can't help it, my gaze drops to her lips again. That red lipstick is going to kill me.

"Toni," she warns.

Our gazes meet, and I see that her eyes are a bit darker than they were moments before. I've seen flashes of that expression this past week, though Audrey's done a good job of quickly snapping back to professional mode.

I drop my voice. "You're thinking it, too. Don't lie."

"I'm thinking of how much I like your hair when it's wild and free."

"Yes, I know."

"You don't play fair," Audrey says.

"And you do?"

"What have I done?"

"Besides the red lipstick?" Audrey blushes slightly. *Thought so.* "You exist, Audrey. In the same space with me. That's it. That's all you have to do."

Audrey's mouth drops open slightly and her expression shifts; her gaze lowers to my lips.

"Audrey, I love your place," Greta says from behind us.

Audrey and I pull apart. I hadn't realized how close we'd gotten and my face flushes with embarrassment. I move to the other side of the kitchen island. As much as I want Audrey, I haven't forgotten Greta's warning. I can do this. I can be professional. I can wait until Audrey finishes the project with the company. My goal over the next few months is to show Greta that I can do this job, and do it well, and to prove to Audrey that I'm not just some one-night stand.

Though looking around Audrey and Willa's townhouse I start to think my initial impression that Audrey is out of my league is spot on. Everything is high end, or at least it seems like it to someone who's slept outside on the trail for most of their life. Their townhouse is in Capitol Hill, a swanky part of Denver, and the interior looks like a spread from the *Architectural Digest* I flip through in my doctor's waiting room. The couches are clean and have all their legs attached. The rug is fluffy and stain free, the colors coordinating with the pillows on the couch and the two facing club chairs. The gas fireplace is lit, and a Christmas tree with multicolored lights in the corner is giving off a festive glow. And then there's the kitchen. Stainless steel appliances shine, the granite countertop is cool and smooth, the cabinets are painted a sleek gunmetal gray. Audrey stands behind the gas stove, stirring the gumbo, looking at ease and completely at home.

Greta's voice jolts me out of my reverie.

"Toni, how's the apartment search going?"

Greta sips her white wine and waits for my reply. Willa and Audrey are waiting for it, too, but I can't speak. I glance back at Greta. It's obvious she's just making conversation, and there's no malice in the question. Little does she know.

"I'm surprised Max hasn't kicked you out yet," Greta continues.

I sneak a glance at Audrey, whose eyebrows have risen to almost her hairline.

"Max?" Willa says.

"Toni's oldest friend. We all grew up together in Aspen. She owns the Dew Drop Inn," Greta says. "Toni stays with Max when she rolls back into town from her trips."

"Do you?" Audrey says.

"I offered to let her stay with me," Greta says. "I have a second bedroom. But apparently she prefers Max's lumpy couch."

Audrey does not look happy, and I can't really blame her. She's definitely not the kind of woman who expects to be having sex in a borrowed bed. God, I am *such* a dirtbag.

"I found a place today," I lie. I haven't had time to look for an apartment this week with work and all. It's amazing how exhausted I am working in an office all day. I've gone back to Max's, shoved food in my mouth, and crashed on the couch and fallen asleep to re-runs of *Law and Order*. Max hasn't seemed eager to kick me out, though our schedules are so different we haven't had time for a conversation. Besides, she likes splitting the bills too much.

"Oh great," Willa says. "Where is it?"

"Um, not far from Max's, as a matter of fact." I mean, I do want to stay in that area, and I can afford it with the salary I'm getting, in addition to the monthly trust-fund allocation Greta and I have received since we each turned twenty-five. "I'm definitely going to need some decorating help." I look around their house and then at Audrey. "Wanna help me?"

"Oh, I didn't do any of this," Audrey says coolly. "This is all Willa."

"I'll be happy to help you, Toni. I love that shit."

"Great," I say, hoping I'm hiding my disappointment. "When I get a move-in date, I'll let you know."

"I'll need to see the space before, as well," Willa says. "Come on, I'll take y'all on a quick tour of the place."

I don't want to go. I want to stay and talk to Audrey, but Audrey says she'll meet us on the deck, and I find myself following Willa and Greta around the townhome. It's spotless, and everything is in its place. This much order and cleanliness makes my teeth itch. But Greta is in love.

"I need to hire you to redecorate my place," Greta says.

Willa waves her hand. "I'll do it for free. Well, maybe a nice bottle of wine now and then."

"You're on."

"It might have to be after I finish this project I'm working on. The company owner is a real micro-manager."

"God, she sounds awful," Greta replies.

"You have no idea," Willa says.

"Is it always this clean?" I ask, feeling surly for no reason I want to admit.

Willa is smiling, but she furrows her brows. Greta scowls behind Willa's back and mouths, "What the fuck, Toni?"

"We just moved in a week ago and we haven't been home much this week, so it's a little more pristine than it normally is. But yeah. Auds and I are both tidy, thank God."

"Ignore Toni," Greta says. "She's used to living in a tent."

"No worries," Willa says, leading us up a final flight of stairs. "We haven't decided what we're going to do up here, yet. Probably a TV room, though neither of us watch much TV. But this. This is why we bought this place." Willa opens a sliding glass door to a rooftop deck with an amazing view of downtown Denver.

"Holy shit," I say.

"Wow," Greta says. "This is amazing, Willa."

It's not a huge space, but it's big enough for a patio couch, two chairs, and a coffee table. Strings of Edison bulb lights are strung back and forth above the space, producing a cozy ambiance that is enhanced by the downtown view and the low music coming from a hidden speaker.

"We bought it for the view," Willa says.

"Great location, spectacular view, lots of space. What a great investment," Greta says.

"That's what we thought, too. If we ever leave Denver, we can rent it out for a nice sum."

"You're thinking of leaving Denver?" I blurt.

"No," Willa says, drawing out the word. "But we might have projects that take us to different parts of the country for extended periods of time."

"Oh, right." I take a huge swig of my beer, feeling the maturity chasm between me and Audrey, Willa, and Greta growing wider every time I open my mouth. I look up, hoping to see the stars but knowing the light pollution will block it.

"I miss it, too," Greta says, looking up at the sky as well. "I love the city, but I miss the mountain sky at night." She looks over at me, smiles and dips her chin ever so slightly, the way she used to when I was a kid trying to hang with her and her friends.

She never said things like, "You got this, sis," because she needed to maintain her competitive, high-achieving reputation at all costs. I never acknowledged it, either, because I needed to make sure the chip on my shoulder that pushed me to be the best stayed firmly in place. It was a silent agreement between the two of us, our secret love language, as fucked up as that sounds. I haven't gotten that signal from Greta in years. My chest swells with affection. I take another drink to swallow the lump in my throat. Greta looks away, and the moment is gone.

Willa lifts a cloth off the coffee table, revealing a meat and cheese platter like the kind you see in fancy wine bars.

"That looks delicious," Greta says. "I love a charcuterie board."

Greta and Willa sit on the couch and chatter on about the different meats and cheeses and debate the best way to build a cracker. Meat or cheese first? Where do you put the jam? They're good-naturedly debating the different merits of the various layers when Audrey arrives, carrying another beer for me and a new bottle of wine.

"Gumbo will be ready in about twenty minutes," Audrey says. She places the wine bottle and her glass on the table and brings the beer to me. She twists it open and hands it to me, her gaze locked on mine. For the life of me, I can't read her. Is she trying to show me that there are no hard feelings about lying to her about the apartment? Or is she just being a good hostess?

I drain my beer and take the one she's offering. "Thanks."

"You're welcome."

I turn towards the view and lower my voice. "About the apartment..."

"Yes, about that," Audrey says. Her eyes are cool as she rests her gaze on mine.

"I'm sorry. I, um, know you thought it was my apartment—"

"And your bed."

"Yes, my bed." I clear my throat. "Max really didn't mind." Audrey raises an eyebrow (she does that a lot and it's not nearly as cute when she isn't trying to seduce me with it). "But what's important is that it was disrespectful to you to not let you know, and I have no excuse except I wasn't thinking straight and—"

"So, Toni," Willa calls. "Audrey says you are more than a pretty face."

Audrey's head whips around toward Willa's voice.

"OK, she didn't say that. But she did say that you have an impressive plan for the adventure division."

"I can't wait to hear it on Monday," Greta says, before taking a bite of a cracker loaded with cheese and jam.

Somehow the cracker doesn't crumble into bits in her hand. How does Greta make everything look so effortless? And why does she look especially beautiful and relaxed tonight when I feel like a taut wire about to snap?

"I want to hear it now. Just the highlights," Willa says. Her legs are pulled up underneath her, and she has one arm on the back of the couch, propping up her head.

Greta leans back as well and crosses one long leg over the other.

Audrey settles into one of the chairs, her arms splayed on the arms like Jean-Luc Picard readying to give the order to *Engage*. She nods her head slightly and sips her wine glass.

I sit on the empty chair, which happens to be nearest Greta, and launch into my plans. As I speak, I'm in my head, imagining the future of Fourteener Adventures, remembering where I was when I had a particular idea, what trail I was hiking, who I was with, the guides from other countries who had been so generous with their time and knowledge, shooting holes in my plans and offering suggestions and advice for how to make something happen in their country. Shaking hands and making promises to collaborate, to respect their culture, community, and their natural resources if and when Fourteener Sports was ready. I mention the foundation idea, and Greta leans forward. She's completely invested now, asking questions, making her own suggestions, until it's a conversation between the two of us and we are feeding off each other's enthusiasm. I glance up and catch Willa and Audrey sharing a smile. Audrey sees me watching, lifts her wine glass in toast, and winks at me.

"Toni, this is amazing," Greta says. "I had no idea your plans were so extensive."

I sit back and sip my beer. "Neither did I, until Audrey started asking me questions and making me put my plans into words."

Greta looks between me and Audrey. "I had no idea," she says again, in a low voice. She inhales and looks at me, a huge grin on her face. "You're going to kill that presentation on Monday."

I tense. "Yeah, about that."

"What's wrong?"

Audrey is on her phone, ignoring us.

"I can't, Gert. I'm so bad at public speaking. My palms literally sweat. My palms have never sweated before."

"Not even when you've cliff-jumped?" Willa asks. "Yes, I've googled you and watched all the crazy shit you do. How are you still alive?"

"Because I don't take risks."

Willa laughs. "Jumping off a cliff only wearing a flimsy wingsuit is a pretty big fucking risk."

"But I've taken all the safety precautions, and double-checked them. By the time I jump, it's almost an afterthought. It's a relief. You've done all the work, now it's time to enjoy the ride."

"And make sure you don't crash into the side of a cliff," Willa says.

"That, too."

"Greta, I just emailed the slide deck Toni put together this week, as well as the supporting detailed business plan. I don't think Toni needs to do a formal presentation yet. She needs more public speaking training. I have no doubt that she will be able to make whatever presentation necessary to sell the tours to corporations eventually."

Greta nods at Audrey and looks at me. I hold my breath,

readying myself for a scolding for not completing the job, for not being good enough.

Greta grabs my arm and squeezes it. "You set your goal too low. You're going to build the biggest adventure tour company in the world, and I'm going to help you do it."

And for the first time in my life, I see admiration in my big sister's eyes.

CHAPTER FOURTEEN

TONI

At the Monday morning department meeting after my impromptu and unintended pitch to Greta, she told everyone about my inspiring direction for the department. She said the pitch deck and business plan would be in everyone's inbox after the meeting and moved on to other business. Later that day, she cleared her schedule, and we went through everything in detail. When she made comments and suggestions, somehow, I didn't get angry, but took her feedback as it was intended. It helped that she was treating me as, if not an equal, at least as the expert in this area. I'd finally impressed my Type A, hard-charging, overachieving, impossible to please sister and my feeling of accomplishment was as thrilling as when I finished climbing my last fourteener. I'm always going to prefer to be outside in nature, but having a goal I believe in, and a sister who doesn't treat me like a loser, makes being in the office easier.

I have Audrey to thank for it all.

That night after dinner I helped her in the kitchen while Greta and Willa cleaned up the deck.

"I knew you could do it," Audrey said, her smile a little smug.

The light bulb went off.

"You planned this."

Audrey shrugged one shoulder and snapped a lid on a glass storage container full of gumbo. "Bombing the presentation in front of a room full of people you've known for years would have done nothing for your confidence and would have probably sent you back into the wilderness for good. So, I gave you and Greta the opportunity to listen to each other on neutral ground."

"You wouldn't like it if I went back into the wilderness for good, huh?" I teased.

Audrey looked at me from beneath her eyelashes, giving me a very stern teacher look. It reminded me of her taking charge and fucking me senseless a mere week earlier.

"I know being out on the trail is your true love. You will never give that up and you shouldn't. You wouldn't be who you are if you did and you would be miserable, and you would hate anyone that asked you to do it. But I think you're intelligent and sharp and so goddamned charming that you will absolutely make Fourteener Trekking a success. But it's going to be tough and tedious at times, and you're going to want to quit more than once. The question is, will you see it through?"

"What do you think?"

"Honestly, I don't know. Are you willing to sacrifice short-term thrills for a long-term satisfaction?"

Her eyes were riveted to mine, and I realized this question wasn't just about Fourteener Trekking.

I opened my mouth to say *Hell yes I am*, but Greta and Willa returned to the kitchen and the moment was over. It's best that we were interrupted because I am certain I would have said something stupid and flirty and immature. I might have even tried to kiss her.

In the two weeks since, I have managed to keep things professional, and I don't think Audrey has any idea about the battle raging inside me every day when I see her. I've never in my life wanted someone like I do Audrey, and it scares the shit out of me. She's warm and slyly funny and so smart it's a little intimidating. She can talk to anyone about anything. I heard her talking to Ned about football (she's a Dallas Cowboys fan, which is almost a deal breaker, but I'll survive) and to Greta about her season tickets to the symphony. When she's in business consultant mode, I sit and marvel at her confidence and intelligence and hope that one day she'll see something in me beyond a one-night stand.

For now, though, I'm focused on doing my job and am trying to be satisfied with grabbing a few minutes of conversation in the break room with Audrey and Willa before the workday officially starts. And laughter. Mostly laughter. Willa is involved, after all. At the end of the day, I find myself in Greta's office, going over my department and my daily progress with my sister. I keep expecting Greta to try to take over the project, to lose faith in my abilities and decide she can do a better job herself. But she never does, and has never even hinted at the idea. She listens to me, tells me what I'm doing well (a lot!), gives suggestions in the areas I'm struggling in (it's a lot, too, but decreasing by the day), and lets me get on with my job.

Inevitably, Audrey and Willa find their way to Greta's office, too, and we sit around and talk business until someone suggests grabbing dinner or, if it's been a hectic day, drinks. OK, the someone in this scenario is usually me or Willa.

The first time Willa suggested drinks, I fully expected Greta to beg off because of more work or a late Pilates class. Instead, she reached into her bottom drawer, pulled out an opened bottle of Maker's Mark, and thunked it on the desk. The three of us stared at her for a beat.

"Are you all going to gape at me or get your mugs?" she asked.

"I don't suppose you have an IPA in there, do you?" I asked.

"It's not a cooler, Toni, it's a drawer."

Willa snorted and Greta's deadpan gaze shifted to her.

Willa couldn't hold back her grin. "Sorry, that was just really funny."

"Imagine if I was *trying* to be funny," Greta said with a straight face.

I knew my sister well enough, though, to see the smallest of cracks in her facade, a softening around her mouth and a twinkle in her eyes.

"Oh, I'll crack you eventually," Willa said.

"You can certainly try," Greta replied.

"I'll get the mugs," Audrey said.

"I'll come with you," I said.

When we were in the hall and well out of earshot, I stage whispered to Audrey, "Were our sisters just *flirting* with each other?"

"They were."

"On *purpose*?" I squeaked.

Audrey laughed. "God, no."

When we returned, Willa said, "Greta has agreed to sing karaoke tonight at the Dew Drop Inn."

"I have done no such thing," Greta said.

"Greta does have a nice voice," I offered.

Greta shot me a look that made her orange-rimmed irises almost glow. I'd been on the receiving end of that expression my entire life and it was still terrifying.

"Or she used to," I added hastily. "I'm sure she totally sucks now."

"You're digging a larger hole every time you open your mouth," Greta said.

"Hit me," I said, shoving my mug in her face. "We could go to Dewey's and not sing," I offer.

Audrey grimaces.

"Afraid you might run into Shae with an E?" I ask.

"Yes," Willa says. "I'm having to do all the errands because she's afraid of running into her."

"Willa," Audrey says sharply.

"Sorry." Willa, for the first time I've known her, looks chastened.

"Is she still texting you all the time?" I ask.

"Yes, but not as often or as... fervently," she says. "I'm not going to the places I might run into her because I don't want to remind her about me."

"How could she forget you?" I ask.

"Oh, I'm sure she's found someone to distract her. She usually does."

"Is this your ex?" Greta asks.

Audrey nods. "Yes."

"You should consider getting a restraining order," Greta says.

"God no," Audrey says. "That would make everything worse, believe me."

"That's what I've been saying, too, Greta. Shae's not going to give up," Willa says. "As soon as she gets tired of her latest side piece she'll come running back."

"I'm going to have to talk to her eventually," Audrey says, "and I will. I've been trying to map out a conversation that allows her to break up with me."

"I'm sorry, what?" Willa says.

"*You* left," I say. "You're broken up. Period. She should respect that."

"But your ex is a narcissist and needs to save face," Greta sums up.

"Precisely," Audrey says.

"That's fucked up," I say.

"Extremely," Willa agrees.

"Thank you all for your concern, but this is my problem and I'll deal with it my way, and in my own time," Audrey says.

Greta nods once and changes the subject. "So, what are you two doing for Christmas? Going home to Texas?"

"No," Audrey says. "I try to avoid going home as much as possible." Willa gives Audrey a sharp look. "We both do. My mother suddenly found Jesus after she discovered I liked girls. She kicked me out of the house."

"She kicked *us* out of the house," Willa said.

"No, she kicked *me* out. You stood by me. She'd take you back in a heartbeat, even now. You were always her favorite."

"Don't remind me. We're a package deal. Always have been, always will be."

Audrey and Willa look at each other with such affection my heart squeezes in my chest. I glance at Greta, whose expression is as inscrutable as always, though she's watching them closely. She catches me watching her and looks caught out for a split second, before smiling warmly at me.

"Tell me, what's Christmas at the Giordani household like?" Willa asks.

"You know, your typical Christmas with a bit of hippy stuff thrown in," I say.

"Such as?" Audrey asks.

"All our ornaments are handmade," I say. "We each make an ornament on Christmas Eve that represents our past year."

"Toni's cheated every year by attaching a ribbon to a pinecone and calling it a day," Greta says.

"The great outdoors," I say, holding out my mug to Greta for another shot.

Greta shakes her head as she pours. "She did a river rock once."

"Yeah, it was a bitch hammering a hole in that for the ribbon," I say. "Never again."

"You know you could have just glued a ribbon to it and been done," Greta says.

I stop with my mug halfway to my mouth. "Why didn't you tell me that when I was doing it?"

"Mom wouldn't let me. She said, *It's the most effort Toni's put into this in years. Leave her to it.*"

"Do you hear that, ladies? How my family treats me?"

"Sounds wonderful to us," Willa says.

"What are your Christmas traditions?" Greta asks.

"We put up our tree and decorations the day after Thanksgiving, as y'all saw, and play Christmas songs for six weeks, at least," Audrey says.

"We chop our tree down a couple of days before Christmas Eve," I say.

"You chop your tree down?" Audrey says.

"We do. Then drink hot chocolate or hot apple cider in the little tree farm cafe after," I say.

"Oh my God it sounds like a Hallmark movie," Willa says. "Audrey and I have always thought about doing that but never have. We have a fake tree."

"OK, that's just blasphemy," I say.

"Who wants to fight that traffic to the mountains?" Audrey says.

"Don't tell me you buy a pine-scented candle to make up for it," I say.

"Yes, I do. And I buy enough pine-scented candles to last the year because I love the scent," Audrey says.

"But not enough to go hiking and smell it naturally," I tease.

"Why would I when I can get it at home while drinking a glass of wine?"

"She makes an excellent point," Willa says.

"What about food? You probably make something super Texan like chicken enchiladas," I say. "Speaking of, I'm starving."

"You're always hungry," Greta says.

"Turkey and dressing and all the fixings," Willa says.

"But that's Thanksgiving dinner," I say.

"We never really had Thanksgiving dinner so the first time we had it we decided we would have it for every holiday," Audrey says.

"Even fourth of July?" Greta asks.

"Actually, yes," Willa says.

"Seriously?" Greta and I say together. We look at each other in astonishment.

"Yep."

"Hang on, you never had Thanksgiving dinner growing up?" I ask.

"Our mother is a terrible cook," Willa says.

"So she found seven recipes that she could cook and we liked and that's what she made. Every day for eighteen years," Audrey says. "Thursday was tuna casserole so by God that's what we were having on Thanksgiving."

Greta and I look at the sisters in horror. "Tuna casserole?" I say. "I've never known anyone who's eaten tuna casserole."

"I'll never eat it again, that's for sure," Willa says, downing her bourbon. She holds out the mug. "Hit me with another shot of whiskey. Audrey, you're driving home."

"I figured," Audrey says.

"Technically it's bourbon," Greta says.

Willa rolls her eyes.

I hold out my mug to Greta. "You can drive me home, too."

"I figured," Greta says.

"I need to say something," Willa says, slurring only slightly.

"I figured *this* was coming, too," Audrey says, a wry smile on her face.

"What?" I ask.

"Willa is a very affectionate drunk," Audrey says.

"There are worse things to be," Willa says. "So, I tell my friends I love them when I'm drunk. It's not a *crime*."

"Are we friends?" Greta asks, deadpan.

"Yes, we are," Willa says. She points at Greta and circles her finger around her face. "I see through that ice queen facade, by the way."

Greta raises an eyebrow and Willa stares at her for a moment, before turning to me and Audrey.

"It's not all the time that Audrey and I like each other's friends and here we are, two sets of sisters"—she looks back at Greta—"all becoming *friends*. Cheers!" Willa holds up her mug.

We all clink our mugs together and drink.

CHAPTER FIFTEEN

AUDREY

"I have a question for you," Willa says.

I park the car in the Fourteener Sports warehouse parking lot. Employees and their families are filing into the building, dressed in festive clothes, for the company holiday party. I kill the car engine and turn down the radio that will continue to play until we open the car doors. Willa and I remove our seatbelts and turn toward each other. Frank Sinatra is imploring us to have a holly, jolly Christmas.

"Shoot," I say.

"If Greta offered you, or us, a job when our contract is up, would you take it?"

"I don't know. Would you?"

"I don't know, either."

"Why do you ask? Has Greta said anything? Hinted at anything?"

Willa scoffs. "No. She's been more reserved than normal since I called her an ice queen."

"It wasn't very nice."

Willa furrows her brows. "Oh, Greta knows I meant it as a compliment. She's having a great time playing the part. She's so distracted by it that she's oblivious to you and Toni mooning over each other all day every day."

"What? No, we aren't."

"Oh my God, yes you are. You do a bit better job of hiding it, but poor Toni. You should see the expression on her face when you're in All-Business Audrey mode."

I reach into my back seat for my purse and sparkly rainbow Santa hat and hope Willa doesn't see me blush.

"Oh, my God," Willa says again. "You *have* noticed. Which is why you go on longer than you should, overexplaining everything. You know Toni thinks it's hot." Willa laughs. "You're torturing the poor woman. Don't you see how she squirms in her chair?"

I press my lips together. "Maybe."

"You are fucking awful," Willa says, but she's laughing. "Telling her you can't be in a relationship yet but winding her up every chance you get. I bet she rubs one off in the bathroom at least once a day."

"Willa!" I say, but I laugh too. "She's not innocent in all this. She knows I love her forearms so she's constantly rolling her sleeves up and flexing her arms and wearing those fucking hiking pants that make her ass look amazing."

"So, she loves you for your mind and you love her for her body."

"No one has said anything about love, and I am attracted to more than her body. If we didn't have this project, would I want something casual with Toni right now? Yes, I would. But we do, so I can't. End of story."

"Uh-huh."

"But you're changing the subject. Why did you ask if I'd take a job with Fourteener Sports? Do you not like being on our own?" It's one of my biggest fears, that Willa quit her job to work with me more out of sisterly solidarity than a real desire to start something from scratch and build it together.

"No, I do. I love this project. But I'm not sure if I love the project or if I love the company. I just... I feel at home here."

I nod. It doesn't surprise me that Willa is drawn to Four-teener Sports and the We're All Family Here vibe that everyone gives off, from Greta down to the janitors (who have worked here longer than Greta). Even before I blew up our family by being gay (my mother's words, not mine) we didn't have a particularly tight family unit. Ever since we left home, Willa has been searching for the family we lost. I've always been happy with just Willa. As much as she claims to the contrary, she misses our mother. The pre-Jesus version one, that is.

"If Greta offers you a job when this is over, you should take it," I say.

"Only if it's the two of us."

"No, Willa. We might be a package deal personally, but professionally we should strike out on our own path if it's a better opportunity. I know how much you've sacrificed for me. Nope." I put a finger on Willa's lips when she starts to speak. "You need to do what's right for you, and only you."

She doesn't look convinced. "Cross that bridge later. Wait until you see the warehouse." She puts her reindeer antlers on her head, and I put on my sequined rainbow Santa hat.

I can't help a gasp of awe when we walk into the warehouse. The main aisle, which is usually full of forklifts moving pallets to and fro, is lined with booths built to look like a snow-covered European village. Each department has their own booth: food, crafts for kids, face painting, and midway games complete with prizes (of a much higher quality than the typical state fair midway junk), with the department Christmas tree beside each one, ready to be judged.

"How in the world did the warehouse get anything accom-plished last week?"

"Honestly, I was here while they did it and I'm not sure.

Everyone knows what needs to be done and does it. It's a pretty well-oiled machine."

At the end of the "street" is a gazebo with an enormous green wingback chair and a Christmas tree with what looks like a hundred presents piled under it. Greta and Toni stand in front of the gazebo with an older couple that can only be their parents and founders of Fourteener Sports.

"Audrey and Willa Adams, these are our parents, Piero and Ingrid Giordani," Greta says.

"What a pleasure to meet you," I say.

"We absolutely love your company," Willa says.

"Thank you," Ingrid says. "We've heard a lot of wonderful things about you from Greta."

"And Toni," Piero says. "She couldn't stop singing your praises, Audrey, for all the help you gave her putting her presentation together."

"Greta was even impressed," Ingrid says, "which is saying something, because she's a hard nut to crack."

"So I've learned," Willa says.

Greta levels Willa with an expression we've come to know well over the last few weeks, part challenge, part amusement, and lately part triumph.

"Toni had all the ideas and did all the work. I was just a guiding hand. She created a solid, achievable ten-year plan," I say.

Mom, Dad, and Greta laugh.

"If you can keep Toni from jumping in with both feet without thinking, then you'll be a miracle worker," Ingrid says.

"Jeez. I love you, too, guys," Toni says.

"We wouldn't be good parents if we didn't tease you a little bit," her dad says. "Keep you humble."

"So, enough talking about how awesome Toni is. We have a problem," Greta says. "Ned fell off a ladder replacing a fuse in his roof lights so he can't be Kris Kringle."

"I'm going to do it," Toni says.

"Not you, Greta?" Willa asks.

"No, I don't like kids enough," Greta admits.

"You don't like kids?" I ask.

Greta shrugs one shoulder. "I haven't been around enough to have much of an opinion. I'm sure when Toni has kids I'll love them, or at least tolerate them."

"Since when am I having kids?" Toni asks.

"Since your sister volunteered you to give us grandkids," Ingrid says.

"It was our Christmas present this year," Piero says.

Toni laughs. When her family's sincere expressions don't change, her laughter dies. "No way. It's the straight daughter's job to give grandchildren, not the lesbian daughter."

"I called it first," Greta says.

"Antonia, you know you would be a much better mother than your sister," Ingrid says.

"Ouch," Willa says around a laugh.

"Hey!" Greta replies. "What does that mean?"

"You *did* just say you don't like kids, Greta," Willa says.

"OK, enough talking about kids that aren't going to happen," Toni says. "I need an elf." She looks at me expectantly.

"You want me to do it?" I ask.

Toni nods.

"Sure. That'll be fun."

"Really?"

"Yeah, why not?"

"You have to wear my Buddy the Elf costume," Toni says.

"Now *I* want to do it," Willa says.

"Not on your life, Rudolph," I say. "I'm sure Greta can find something for you to do."

"Absolutely. Come with me."

"You better be leading me to the bar," Willa says.

Greta shakes her head, but there's a hint of a smile behind it. "There is no bar."

"Before we get distracted," Ingrid says, "we want to invite you two to spend Christmas with us in Aspen."

Willa and I stare at the Giordanis in surprise, then at each other. Christmas with the Giordanis? Our clients?

"What did you have in mind? For us to drive down for a couple of hours on Christmas Day?" I ask. Surely not. Traffic on I-40 west of Denver will be a nightmare. I can't imagine anyone asking someone to do that. I don't want to do that. How in the world can we turn this down, though?

"Oh, no. We would like for you to come for a few days. Say Monday through Boxing Day?" Piero says.

"Oh, we couldn't impose like that," I say.

"It's not an imposition, trust me," Ingrid says.

"We've been talking about it for a couple of weeks," Greta says. "But didn't mention it because Mom wanted the invitation to come from her."

"It's harder to turn her down in person," Toni says.

Would accepting this invitation cross a line? Would it compromise my and Willa's ability to be objective with the project, give criticism when it's warranted? I think about all the evenings after work the four of us have spent together these last two weeks and realize that somehow we've already crossed the line from colleagues to friends. If I'm honest, I crossed a line when I unwittingly slept with Toni two days before the project started.

Oh Christ, do Ingrid and Piero know about that? Their expressions are open and friendly. No suspicion at all. They must not. That's a relief. But how in the hell am I going to spend days and nights with Toni and keep my attraction from Greta, Ingrid, and Piero? Lord knows Toni doesn't have a poker face.

One look at Willa and I know that she wants to go. Desperately. I would do anything for my sister, including being sexually frustrated for days on end.

"They're communicating telepathically," Toni whispers to her parents. "Willa told me about it. Pretty fascinating."

I smile and nod at Willa, and it's decided.

"Don't feel obligated or put on the spot if you have plans," Piero says.

"Our plans are to spend Christmas with each other, like every year," I say.

"We can do that with you, as long as you let us help you with cooking and stuff," Willa says.

"Of course," Ingrid says. "Drive down the day after tomorrow and stay through Boxing Day. We are looking forward to sharing the holidays with you."

"We are, too, Mrs. Giordani," I say.

"Ingrid, please." She leans close and stage whispers, "It's actually Danzig, dear. I kept my name, but we used Giordani in promotional materials early on to make it easier and never stopped."

"Got it."

"Let's get this party started," Piero says.

"Greta, take me to the bar," Willa says.

Greta leads Willa away. "This is a kid-friendly party, Willa," I hear Greta say.

"Why do you think I need alcohol?" Willa says. She looks at me over her shoulder and winks broadly.

Even though I've told her multiple times now that I don't need her to be my wing-woman and lure Greta away, at least not until after the project is over, she doggedly continues to do her best to distract Greta from focusing on me and Toni. She's going to have to work overtime this weekend.

"She's doing that on purpose, isn't she?" Toni asks.

"Winding Greta up? Yes, yes she is."

"I love her so much," Toni says. "Come on. Let's get you changed."

She leads me to the back of the warehouse to a break room that's shabby, but spotless.

"We're in a break room," I tease. "Are you going to spill cider all over me?"

"Not this time, I don't think." She takes the costume off the table and hands it to me. "Here you go."

It really is a Buddy the Elf costume, complete with elf shoes and all. Toni is taller than I am so it's not a great fit, but I look passable. When I walk out of the bathroom, Toni is standing in the middle of the room in nothing but red Santa pants, hiking boots, and a sports bra. My stomach flutters at the sight of her toned abs. I should have given them more attention when I had the chance. I lick my lips, partly from memories and partly from the delayed gratification when I finally do get a chance to trace those ridges with my lips and tongue, just as Toni looks up and sees me.

"That looks so much better on you than me," Toni says. "You look like Peter Pan with your short hair."

"Thanks." I nod toward her almost naked torso. "You better cover those up before someone comes in and sees me ogling you."

"Ogling?" Toni's clear blue eyes spark with mischief. "How unprofessional, Miz Adams."

"Says the woman flashing her abs."

"What? These old things?" Toni holds her arms above her head and rolls her abs up and down in a mockingly sexy dance move.

I can't help but laugh. "Of course you know how to do that."

"It took me months to master it."

"Put those things away before someone gets hurt."

Toni laughs and zips up the coat, and buckles the belt.

"I love how you make me laugh," I blurt.

Toni looks up at me in surprise, her eyes still sparkling. "This isn't normal? Laughing together?"

"Not in my experience, no. I didn't realize I wanted it until —" I almost say *I had it*, but I don't really have it yet, do I? "I've only had it with Willa."

Toni moves closer and puts her hand over her heart. "I promise, if I ever get the chance, I will make it my mission in life to make you laugh. At least fifteen times a day."

"That's a strangely specific number."

"It's my favorite."

"Any reason?"

"Greta's is seven and I always had to be twice as good as she is, plus one."

"Oh my God, are you that competitive in everything?"

Toni leans forward and drops her voice. "Have you forgotten about fair ups?"

God no, I think. I want to move closer, have to physically restrain myself from pulling Toni to me and crushing my mouth against hers, just as I've had to do for the last month whenever she's looked at me like that. I'm not sure what Toni sees, but I see flashes of what could be: lazy mornings in bed, browsing weekend markets hand in hand, cooking for her, laughing together and yes, I've even tried to imagine going on hikes with her. It's a testament to Toni's charisma, and our chemistry, that I picked up a hiking boot on my last visit to a Fourteener Sports store. I put it down quickly because it was big, bulky, and ugly. But I have looked, tried to imagine wearing them, hiking up some godforsaken rock-strewn, root-covered trail with a thousand-foot drop off into a rushing river on one side of the narrow trail and a slick rock face with no handholds on the other.

Toni laughs. "Please tell me you weren't just thinking about kissing me."

"What?"

"You just grimaced." Toni contorts her face into a pained expression.

"I did not look like that."

"You did, and if that's your reaction to kissing me, I'm in deep trouble."

"No, I wasn't. I mean, yes, I was. At first. Then I started thinking about hiking."

Toni's grin widens. "We'll parse out why thinking about kissing me led you to hiking later, but I *have* to know what you were imagining."

"A narrow trail with a slick rock face on one side and a very steep drop off into a roaring river on the other," I say.

Toni rubs her chin and gets a comically thoughtful expression on her face. She nods. "You weren't thinking about hiking."

"I was definitely thinking about hiking."

"No, it's a metaphor."

"Oh, is it?"

"For us. Our relationship. On the one side it's a rock-solid friendship. On the other is a big old roaring river of passion."

"Passion?" I'm trying to stop a grin from breaking across my face.

"Um, yeah. Don't even act like you've forgotten about our night together. Passion, Audrey. Insane attraction. Unresolved sexual tension that makes Sam and Frodo look like a crush."

"Sam and Frodo?"

"You don't like that example?"

"I'm thinking Sherlock and Watson."

"OK, that's legit. Mulder and Scully?"

"Gillian Anderson and anyone she shares a screen with."

"God, that woman could step on me like a bug," Toni says.

"Hard same."

"Anyway!" Toni says. "My point is that your mind going from kissing me to a horror hiking scenario that I would *never* put you in, at least not until we've been together for a few years—"

"I *knew* it."

"It's all just a stand-in for your fear about us." Toni steps forward and takes my hands. "You don't have to be scared of me, or us. I respect that you need time. It might be the hardest thing I've ever done, and I jump off cliffs wearing a bodysuit with wings, so that's saying something. But I promise. I'll never do anything to hurt you."

I'm not sure if I believe her, that's a big promise to make, but there is no doubt in my mind that Toni wholeheartedly believes it.

She's very close. "Do you know how hard it is working with you?"

You have no idea.

"Is it? I can't tell," I say instead.

"Then you're blind as a bat, Audrey Adams. I feel like all I do is stare at you."

Stare at me *is* all Toni does when we're around each other, but if I acknowledge that I've seen it, if I break even a little, I will push her up against the wall and kiss her until she forgets her name.

"Every day, every time I see you, I want to kiss you so much it's almost a physical pain," she says.

I swallow hard, reminding myself of all the reasons kissing Toni is a bad idea, the least of which is, if I kiss her, I won't be able to stop and there is a warehouse full of families on the other side of the unlocked break-room door.

"This isn't easy for me either, Toni."

She raises her eyebrows, clearly stunned.

"Oh, come on. That can't be a surprise," I say.

"I'm surprised you admitted you want to kiss me."

"That I want to kiss you?" I laugh. If she only knew. "You

won't have to wait forever. We won't have to wait forever. Six or seven months."

"OK, just so we're clear here, do you mean that you want to, like, date me eventually?"

"Yes, I do." I smile. "Merry Christmas."

Toni's grin widens. "That's the best Christmas gift ever."

"You're welcome. Now. Enough flirting. Let's go put smiles on a bunch of kids' faces."

"Sure, but for the record, there's no such thing as too much flirting."

I hold the door open for her and roll my eyes good-naturedly. "Simmer down, Casanova."

"I think you mean *Santa*nova."

"Oh my God, that was awful," I say, but can't help laughing.

"Yeah, I know," Toni says, extremely proud of herself, none-theless.

The children in line to see Santa start cheering and screaming when they see Toni. She immediately bellows a deep, "Ho, Ho, Ho!" and something deep inside me stirs.

CHAPTER SIXTEEN

AUDREY

I was wrong. There were at least two hundred presents under that Christmas tree and we've handed out nearly all of them, thank God. Watching Toni play Santa, letting kids sit on her lap and tell her what they want for Christmas with a sweet, steady smile and affection is incredibly attractive. Toni is effortlessly charming, but her charm is rooted in kind-heartedness, selflessness that you see less and less these days. Greta, despite her talk of not liking kids, is patient and sweet with every single child that comes up to give her a hug, and they all come up to give her a hug. All four of the Giordanis receive hugs from every family member. They have conversations with all of them, focusing on each, making them seem like the only people in the room. If I'm exhausted after merely smiling and handing kids presents, I can't imagine how tired the Giordanis are.

We're down to only a dozen or so presents when I look up to see where the end of the line is and see the last person I expect chatting with Piero.

Shae.

Shae grins and waves. She's wearing her black-rimmed

glasses and a newsboy hat I bought her. She looks good, but Shae always looks good. But this time there's no desire, no quickening of my pulse. All I feel is frustration, anger, and confusion. What the hell is she doing here? And why is she talking to Piero?

Willa notices I'm holding up the line and follows my gaze. Before I can say anything or move, Willa is off, a thunderous expression on her face.

Oh shit.

I grab the nearest person I know and ask them to take over for me for a moment and walk as quickly as possible, but there is no way I'm catching my sister. I see Piero's expression go from polite professionalism to confusion as soon as Willa opens her mouth.

"—got some fu— nerve coming here. What do you think you're doing?" Willa says.

I put my hand on Willa's arm. She's vibrating with anger and I'm reminded of the scene fifteen years earlier when my mother kicked me out of the house. Willa means well, but right now she has tunnel vision, and that tunnel is bright red with anger and pointed directly at Shae. She's forgotten, or doesn't care, where we are. That no matter what the fuck Shae is doing here, we have to maintain our professionalism. We aren't employees, we're contractors, and guests at this Christmas party. We *cannot* make a scene.

I should be the one who's angry, and I probably will be later. But a calmness settles over me. This conversation was going to happen eventually. Might as well get it over with.

"What the hell are you doing here, Shae with an E?" Toni says in full Santa regalia, including fake beard.

"Toni," Piero says, a warning in his voice.

"Toni," Shae says and looks her up and down. "You look better in biker drag."

"I'll walk you out, Shae," I say. "Willa, will you take over for me with the kids? Excuse us." I move forward quickly, try to grab Shae by the elbow to turn her around, but she takes my hand. It's more important that I get her out of the building and save as much face as possible, so I don't release her hand, but tighten my grip and pull her along. Once outside I search the parking lot for her car. I pull her towards it.

"I'm coming, you don't have to drag me," Shae says.

I release her hand and walk the remainder of the way. At her car, I turn and cross my arms over my chest. "What do you think you're doing, coming here like this?"

"I wanted to talk to you."

"I don't want to talk to you. That should be pretty obvious by now." Shae opens her mouth to respond but I hold up my hand. "I've said all I have to say, all there is to say. You need to leave. Now."

"No. I'm not leaving until you tell me why."

"Oh my God, you're joking, right?" Shae starts to speak but I keep going. "One of the reasons was hanging all over you that night at Dewey's. She's one of a half dozen reasons, that I *know* of. I'm sure there's more."

"That wasn't what it looked like."

I roll my eyes. "Why do you even care, Shae? You were obviously never satisfied with being monogamous. Now you can do what you want to do with whomever, whenever. Is this all about saving face?"

"Saving face?"

"It must be humiliating that I left you. Big blow to your ego and reputation."

"You didn't leave me."

I laugh. "OK, fine. Now's your chance. Break up with me."

"What?"

"Break up with me. That way you can say you were the one who tossed me aside instead of the other way around."

"But you're who I want."

"If I was the one you wanted you wouldn't have cheated on me multiple times."

"Those women didn't mean anything to me."

"Well, they meant something to *me*," I shout.

"Calm down, Audrey."

"Oh my God," I say, and walk away. I see Toni, Willa, and Greta standing close enough to hear, but far enough to not interfere. Seeing them standing there, supporting me, steels my resolve. I hold my hand out to make sure they don't move closer because this is my fight. I turn around. "How did you know where I was?"

"I knew where your new project was, so I guessed."

"You guessed I'd be at the warehouse? On a Saturday at four p.m."

Shae's face goes blank. She's obviously trying to think of a lie.

"Are you tracking my phone?" I ask.

"No. You changed all your passwords."

"So you tried." What in the hell could she be using to track me? A chill goes down my spine. I'm staring at her Mercedes, bought from the same dealership as mine, containing the same software. I gasp. "You're tracking my car. That's low, even for you."

"I'm going to kill her," I hear Willa say. I don't turn around. I have to hope that Toni and Greta will hold her back.

"I'm sorry, Audie. I had to talk to you. I want another chance."

"I've told you no a hundred times."

"Why not?"

I've told her *why* a hundred times. Maybe a hundred and one will be the magic number. "Because you're a cheater, a manipulator, and a gaslighter and I'm done. Really done this time."

"I'm none of those things."

I shake my head and try to walk away. Again. She grabs my elbow. I wrench it from her grasp, and cross my arms over my chest.

"I mean, I know you believe that," Shae says. "Which is why I'm going to therapy. To really interrogate myself on why you think these things about me. I've been three weeks in a row. I'm really excited about this therapist. She gets me, you know."

We've been here before. Too many times to count. She promises to change (though she never admits to being at fault or having a fault), goes to therapy for a few sessions, loves the new therapist. She made it to the sixth appointment once, which was a record. As soon as the therapists stop listening and start digging, asking Shae to be vulnerable, to admit some part in our problems, Shae leaves and never goes back. And then she cheats. Even Freud wouldn't be able to get Shae Baker to make it past six therapy appointments.

Why didn't I leave earlier? I don't like to fail, that's one reason, the reason all the other reasons stem from. Shae knows me so well that she was always able to push the buttons that would make me doubt myself, the comments, turns of phrase and the subtext that would make me believe that the real problem was I wasn't trying hard enough to make our relationship work. I knew it was a lie. I knew she was manipulating me. But she wore me down. Every time. And I stayed.

This time, it won't work. I've had a glimpse of other possibilities, other futures. It's time to end this once and for all.

Shae looks over my shoulder and smirks at Toni, Willa, and Greta. Willa's expression is thunderous. Toni looks angry and gobsmacked. Greta's brows are furrowed as she types something on her phone.

"Back off, Willa," Shae says. "This doesn't have anything to do with you."

"You did *not* just say that to me," Willa says, and lunges forward.

Greta holds my sister back and Toni moves closer, an extra layer of protection between Willa and Shae.

"You need to leave, Shae," Toni says in a firm voice.

Shae looks at Toni, Greta, and Willa and laughs. "Seriously, Audrey? Call off your attack dogs."

"We aren't attack dogs, we're her friends," Toni says. "We heard what she said but you apparently didn't. She doesn't want to talk to you."

"We were talking just fine before you interrupted," Shae says.

"Enough!" I say. I turn to my friends. "Can y'all please go inside? I'll be right there."

"I'm not leaving you out here with her. She might kidnap you," Willa says.

"Always the drama queen," Shae says.

"One more word out of you and I am going to fuck you up," Willa says through clenched teeth.

"OK," Greta says, turning around and literally pushing Willa backwards. "Let's give them some space."

Toni glances between me and Shae and says, "You sure?"

"Yes, I'm sure."

Toni nods. I can tell that the last thing she wants to do is to leave me, but she backs away. None of them go inside, though. Greta has a firm enough grip on Willa that I don't have to worry about her launching herself at Shae.

I'd managed to keep my distance from my ex, but now she steps close enough that I can smell her cologne. I hate the way my body responds to it, to her scent. Chemistry was never a problem with us. Until I realized that I somehow wasn't enough for her.

"Audie," she says in the voice I know so well. It's low and

intimate, the voice she used when she was either fucking me or trying to manipulate me.

But instead of making me go weak in the knees, it snaps me back to reality and I cross my arms over my chest. "Why now?"

"What?"

"Why today of all days did you suddenly remember that you have access to my car GPS?"

Shae motions for me to come with her. "Let's go talk privately."

I laugh. "Not on your life. I want everyone to hear your answer."

"Audrey..."

Adrenaline courses through my body. I barrel on. "You've texted consistently, but they seemed perfunctory. As if you felt like you should *try* to get me back but didn't really want to."

"That's not true."

"Yeah, it kinda is," Willa says. "She showed me the texts."

I love my sister but Jesus Christ. I turn. "Willa, *shut up.*" I glare at Shae, arms crossed. "You texted me to try to keep me on the hook so if things didn't work out with your latest girlfriend, you could come back to me."

Shae chuckles and tries for innocence. "Audrey, I'm not that manipulative."

I laugh. "Oh, yes you are. Did your girlfriend break up with you?" When Shae doesn't react, I continue. "Or maybe not, but she left for Christmas." Shae looks sheepish now. "And you don't want to be alone."

"We're so good together."

"I've told you over a dozen times in a dozen different ways that this is over and you *just won't listen* to me. It's exhausting. I've tried to be nice, because of all we had together, the good times, and I don't want to hurt you. But I cannot take this anymore." I inhale deeply and look her in the eyes. "I don't love you anymore. It is over. I will never come back. There is nothing in the world that you could do or say that would make me take you back. Do you understand?"

"No, we can make this work."

"Oh my God, that's it," Toni says and moves so quickly I can't stop her.

She's got Shae by the arm and Shae is not having it. She rips her arm from Toni's grasp. I can tell where this is going, so I move between them.

"Stop it. We're in public, for God's sake." I turn to Shae and step back, putting distance between us, and pushing Toni behind me. "I've been patient with you, Shae, but I'm done. You're harassing me, at my place of work. What are you thinking, stalking me here?"

"Stalking you? I'm not stalking you."

"You tracked my car, Shae. That's stalking. It's also sad and desperate."

"And pathetic," Willa says.

I don't scold her because I see Shae's eyes widen slightly. Finally, something is hitting home.

Employees and their wives and kids are exiting the warehouse, loaded down with presents and baked goodies. They wave and say goodbye, while eyeing us all with curiosity.

Maybe public shaming will work. Nothing else has.

"When word gets around town that you made a scene at a business function about personal business," I say. "Well, wow. Your reputation is going to take a pretty brutal hit."

Shae's eyes widen further.

"I mean *I* wouldn't say anything, but—" I wave my hand at the stream of people leaving, and at Greta, Willa, and Toni.

Shae regains her composure quickly and she scoffs. "Please, no one would believe it."

"Yet here you are, begging me to take you back. Shae Baker having to beg a woman to be with her." I pull out my phone and wave it around. "It's usually 'video or it didn't happen' but I think audio will work, too." Shae's eyes narrow. "Or just leave me alone and this stays between us."

"You didn't record this."

"Do you want to take that chance?"

Shae studies me. I have no idea what my expression says, but I hope it's something along the lines of, *Dare me, bitch.*

Shae opens her car door. "You're going to regret this, Audrey. You think this *trail guide* will make you happy?" She gestures to Toni and laughs. "In a month or so, when you get bored with this loser, don't bother crawling back to me. I wouldn't take you back if you begged me."

"I wouldn't beg you for water if I was dying of thirst," I say.

Shae gets in the car, slams the door, and starts the engine. I turn to walk away, relief flooding through me.

Shae rolls down her window. "Hey."

Reluctantly, I turn around. Of course, Shae needs to get the last word in.

"The promotion you lost? I might have let slip at a happy hour with your CEO that I was being recruited for a job in California and that you were excited to go with me."

My stomach drops. "That's a lie."

"Not technically. I did get a call, once, about a job in California. But I wasn't interested." She winks at me. "Sorry about that."

With that, she peels out of the parking lot.

My mouth gaping open, I turn to my sister and friends. I'm too stunned to speak.

"Why does that not surprise me?" Willa says.

"Why would she do something like that?" Toni asks.

"I don't kn—" I start.

"Oh yeah you do," Willa says. "If Audrey would have gotten that promotion, it would have been a bigger job and better title than Shae's, and she couldn't stand that."

"Good lord," Greta says.

"Jesus," Toni says. "Even I'm not that competitive."

"You were bluffing about recording Shae, weren't you?" Willa asks.

"Yeah."

"Too bad. She deserves to have that blasted out on TikTok," Willa says.

"That's the least of what she deserves," Toni says.

"Hey." Willa puts her hands on my shoulders and makes me look her in the eye. "Forget about that lost promotion. It wasn't because of you or anything you did. You're fine. What's important is you are rid of Shae once and for all. How do you feel about that?"

I inhale, paying attention to how I feel physically. Elated, like a weight has been lifted from my shoulders. Light. I smile at my sister. "Relieved and happy."

"Good girl," Willa says. "Now, let's wrap up this party so we can have some wine."

I walk into the warehouse in a daze. Could it really be over? Hopefully the prospect of public shame will do the trick on Shae. The revelation of her sabotage of my promotion, seeing the shocked expression on my face, will make her feel like she won the war. How could she have done that to me? To anyone? How could my CEO have taken her word and not talked to me about it before making a decision? Maybe it had been less about me blowing the whistle on an inappropriate affair, and more about the fact that I didn't like corporate politics. I wasn't a kiss-ass, preferring to let my work speak for itself. Because I didn't play the game, any hint that I might not be committed to the company for the long haul would have been enough to let them choose one of the "boys." Did I really care? No. Like Willa said, I'm fine. Better than fine. I love this project and the people at Fourteener Sports.

Then, there's Toni.

Sweet, funny, respectful, incredibly sexy Toni. I asked her

to back off and she did. She believed in me enough to let me fight my own battle. I can't really blame her for losing her patience at the end. Shae can be infuriating. And, as shallow as this is, she looks absolutely adorable in the oversized Santa costume. Watching her be so kind and energetic for hours with all the kids and families, when I know she had to be exhausted, was just... it shows the kind of person she is deep down. The kind of woman I want to spend more time with.

Toni and I head to the break room to change. When the door closes behind us, Toni says, "I'm sorry I jumped in there at the end. You were handling everything perfectly, it's just..." She runs her hands through her hair.

"Don't apologize," I say. "You were amazing. Perfect."

"Me? I didn't do anything. You were the badass."

"You did. When I told you I could handle it, you listened to me, and respected me. You backed off when I know you wanted to tear Shae limb from limb."

"Oh my God, so much. You could tell?"

I hold up my thumb and forefinger so they're almost touching. "A little." I laugh. God, I'm so happy right now. I'm free of Shae, I love my job, Willa is happy, I've got an amazing friend in Greta, and an incredibly kind, sexy woman standing in front of me who looks at me like a Christmas puppy and makes me laugh. "Have I told you lately how much I love how you make me laugh?"

"A couple of times."

"I do. It's very sexy." I look at Toni's lips and think, *Oh, damn it to hell.* I grab the back of her head and crush our mouths together.

I've caught her off guard, but she recovers quickly, and we are devouring each other as if it's been years since we've touched and not three weeks. My arousal pulses deep in my core, and I'm having a hard time remembering why I've been denying myself this. Why I've been denying both of us. We're adults. There's no reason we can't have a little fun, like Toni suggested the night we slept together. We will have to be careful, keep it secret, but the way Toni looks at me, the way she's kissing me, tells me that she will do whatever it takes to have this, to feel this. So will I.

Toni breaks the kiss, pushes me back to arm's length. "Wait. We can't."

"What? Why not?"

"I understand now, Audrey. Why you need time. It was... awful to see you go through that. Has Shae been emotionally abusive the entire time you were together?"

My head jerks back. "What?"

"That was emotional abuse, Audrey."

"Shae just doesn't like to lose."

"I wrote the book on being competitive and not wanting to lose. That is *not* what that was."

I move out of her embrace and cross my arms over my chest and instinctively defend Shae and the dynamic of our relationship. "I don't think you should judge Shae or our relationship based on five minutes of seeing us together. That was Shae at her absolute worst. She isn't always like that." As the words spill out of my mouth seemingly of their own accord, the other side of my brain screams, *Audrey, what the hell? She was exactly like that, why are you defending her? She sabotaged your career!*

I stop. Toni's expression is a mixture of stunned and confused. She tries to put her hands in her pockets and realizes she's dressed like Santa. I look down and realize I'm still wearing this stupid Buddy the Elf costume.

"OK, Audrey," she says, holding her hands out in a placating gesture. "I know this is... well, like the high you feel after a battle. I know you just want to have a little fun, and I did offer that the night we were together. I'm just not sure I can do that now."

The door to the break room opens and Willa peeks her head

in. One look at us and she huffs. "You aren't changed yet? I've somehow convinced Greta to sing karaoke at Dewey's. We need to go before she changes her mind."

"Hell, yeah we do," Toni says. She grabs her clothes and follows Willa out the door without looking at me.

I watch the door close behind her and wonder what the hell I'm going to do now.

CHAPTER SEVENTEEN

TONI

Try as I might, I can't get Shae's jab out of my mind.

In a month or so, when you get bored with this loser…

I know Shae is a douchebag and said that to wind me up, but I didn't need to be reminded that Audrey is out of my league.

"Toni, help me get the next round." Greta grabs my arm and pulls me to the bar.

I knew it was only a matter of time before Greta got me alone. Max sees us coming and her eyes light up in the very uncharacteristic way they do when Max sees Greta. Max is pulling our beers out of the cooler before we order. In a move honed over years of bartending at her parents' bar before opening this one.

"Only three, Max. Topo Chico for me," Greta says. "I'm driving to Aspen tonight. One beer is my limit."

"Cool. You can be my DD," I say.

"The more things change," Greta says.

Max opens three beers in quick succession. Greta slides one towards me.

"Audrey really undersold how toxic Shae is."

"You can hardly blame her," I say.

"Did you have any idea?"

"An inkling from a couple of things she said that night, but it was so much worse than I expected." I take a long pull of my beer. God, it tastes good.

Max puts her forearms on the bar and leans in.

"Look, I know the chances of you listening to me are slim," Greta says.

"What? That's not true, I listen to you."

Greta rolls her eyes and tries to hand her credit card to Max, who waves it away.

"I'll be right back," Max says before walking off to serve other customers.

"Be careful, Toni. I like Audrey a lot. But we just got a glimpse of the relationship she's getting out of and you do not want to get in the middle of that right now. Audrey needs time to recover from what sounds, and looked, like an emotionally abusive relationship."

"Yeah, I told her that too. She denied it."

"Denied she needed time or denied it was abusive?"

"The second. Well, both, really."

Greta's eyebrows rise, waiting for me to elaborate. No way I'm telling her Audrey kissed me in the break room. She pours her Topo Chico into the glass of ice and squeezes the lime in it. I can see in her eyes that she's processing everything. She sips the fizzy mineral water out of the tiny brown stirring straw, and puts down the glass.

"It would be hard for someone like Audrey to admit to themselves that they've been so thoroughly manipulated, and by someone they cared about."

"Yeah, probably," I say.

Greta looks into the near distance, deep in thought.

"What?"

"I just wonder how this will affect the project."

"Jesus, have some compassion, Greta."

She glares at me. "I do have compassion for her, but I'm also a CEO responsible for a multimillion-dollar business with hundreds of employees across the country counting on me. So, excuse me if I consider how the lead contractor's emotional state will affect a pivotal moment in our company's history."

"You don't have to worry about me fucking anything up. I told her that I realized now why she needs space."

"Is that what you want?" Greta asks.

"Hell, no. I think about her constantly and I want to be with her every moment of every day. But that's what she needs, and I'm going to respect it. I don't want to be a rebound." I look Greta in the eyes. "I want this to last."

Greta raises her eyebrows. "That's very mature of you."

"Yeah, well this *trail guide* isn't a total idiot."

"Don't listen to Shae."

"She's right, though. Audrey is out of my league."

"Yes, she is," Greta says, twisting the knife that Shae stabbed into my heart earlier. "But she won't be forever." She turns completely toward me and looks me dead on in the eyes. "I think Audrey is great for you, Toni. She challenges you in a completely different way than you've ever been challenged, and you've risen to it. The work you've done so far has been impressive. The way Audrey read your strengths and weaknesses and figured out a way for you to succeed?" Greta shakes her head in amazement.

Max walks back up to us and leans on the bar. "What did I miss?"

Greta's focus is still on me. "I'm not an idiot, Toni. I've seen the way you look at her, and the way she looks at you."

My heart flutters at that. So, I *haven't* been reading into Audrey's expressions what I want to see if Greta sees it, too. Excitement courses through me. OK, fine. It's lust coursing through me.

"And I'm not looking forward to watching you moon over her for four days in Aspen," says Greta.

"They're coming to Aspen?" Max asks.

"For Christmas," I say.

Greta continues. "I probably don't show it as much as I should, but I care about you, Toni. I think there's as good a chance that Audrey is perfect for you as there is that she will break your heart, and I don't want to see you get hurt."

"I think it's too late for that," I say.

Greta heaves a huge sigh. "Whatever happens, do not let the fallout affect the company, your job, or Audrey's project."

"It won't. I promise."

"Good. Because I've had Finance run the numbers and if we achieve what you want to with the adventure division, it's going to be a huge revenue stream for us, and it will also increase sales in our core areas."

Leave it to Greta to bring it all back to money. I'm about to call her out on it but she keeps speaking.

"But Mom and Dad only got me to agree to bring you into corporate if I had the authority to fire you without their interference, and if you fuck up this project because you're sleeping with Audrey, I will fire you." She takes her drink, and one beer, and walks back to the table.

CHAPTER EIGHTEEN

AUDREY

I watch Toni and Greta at the bar, obviously in a tense conversation, no doubt about what happened a few hours ago. The four of us have spent the last hour listening to bad karaoke and drinking beer, talking about lighthearted subjects.

"The answer is yes," Willa says.

I tear my focus away from the bar and lift my beer bottle almost to my lips. "What was the question?" I ask, downing the lukewarm dregs of my IPA.

"Are they talking about me. *Me* in this question being you."

"I gathered," I say. I set the empty bottle on the table with a clink. "There's something else." I tell Willa about the kiss in the break room and how Toni ended it.

"So now you want her, but she doesn't want you," Willa says.

I bristle. "I wouldn't put it exactly like that."

"Sounds like it to me."

"I love you, Willa, but you don't always have to be so blunt."

Willa rolls her eyes. "Yes, I do. Would you really want to be with a woman who witnessed that dumpster fire and then wanted to jump right into bed with you? You know who would do that? Shae, that's who. Toni is respecting the boundary you set the night you two fucked like rabbits—"

"Really, Willa."

"—and you're too horny to see her rejection for what it is."

"What is it?"

"Love, dumbass."

"I'm not ready for that."

"Toni is smart enough to get that, which is why she put the brakes on." Willa watches me and must not like what she sees in my expression. She leans forward. "Instead of being pissed that you aren't going to get laid, why don't you appreciate the fact that you have a woman who is putting you and what you need first."

I inhale. "You're right. Of course, you're right."

"I usually am," Willa says. "I don't know if it's this new career direction we're on, being out of that toxic bitch Shae's orbit, or Toni, but you've been happier in the last few weeks than I've seen you in a long time. A *long* time. I've finally gotten my sister back and you better believe I'm going to do whatever I can to make sure she sticks around."

"I could say the same about you," I say, and glance at Greta and Toni, who are still in deep conversation.

Greta looks our way and Willa motions for another beer. Greta nods and holds up one finger. Willa returns her attention to me, and I see a small smile on her face. She raises her eyebrows.

"What?"

"Nothing at all."

Greta returns to the table and hands Willa a beer.

"Did you have to go harvest the hops?" Willa teases.

Greta sits down next to her with a chuckle. "Something like that."

"Oh my God I'm having flashbacks to college," I say.

"What do you mean?" Greta asks.

"Don't listen to her," Willa says.

"Whenever we would go out, Willa always got drinks bought for her and I never did."

"Not true," Willa says.

"It's totally true, and here we are, yet again."

Greta points to Toni, who has arrived with my beer.

"See?" Willa says.

"What did I miss?" Toni asks.

"Audrey is about to explain to me how her twin sister always had a free drink in her hand and she didn't," Greta says.

"People *like* me," I say. "Everyone *loves* Willa."

"I've heard this before," Toni says. "Didn't believe it then, don't believe it now."

"Toni's right, though you're probably a smidge biased." Willa winks at Toni.

"Touché," Toni says.

"Hey, Willa promised to get on stage and sing an ABBA song," Greta says, smirking.

"Funny, that's exactly what Willa said about you," Toni says.

"You're going to have to buy me something stronger than a beer to get me on that stage," Willa says.

"Don't listen to her, Greta. She loves singing karaoke and ABBA is her favorite," I say.

"I knew it," Greta says.

"Audrey, shh. I'm trying to get more free drinks. Is it any wonder she didn't get them in college?"

"So you're admitting it!" I say, laughing.

A duet starts singing Sonny and Cher, drowning out cross-table conversation. So I turn to Toni and catch her looking at me with the Christmas puppy expression, one that makes my stomach go soft and gooey, before she schools her face into something almost passive. Maybe the conversation between her and Greta was better than I thought. Still, Willa's right. I should appreciate that Toni is respecting me and respect her boundary in return.

"Looked like a deep conversation at the bar," I say. "Everything OK?"

"Yep. Greta is just doing her big sister thing."

"You two seem to have been getting along really well over the last few weeks."

"We are, and I have you to thank for it." She clinks her bottle against mine and takes a long drink.

"Me?" I try not to watch the muscles in her neck contract, but it's difficult when I know what she smells like just behind her ear and how her long neck feels against my lips.

"Yes. You set me up to succeed with the non-pitch pitch. I think Greta is finally seeing me as an adult instead of her bratty little sister who's everyone's favorite."

"So modest," I tease.

We smile at each other and contentment washes over me. It usually takes me days, and multiple naps, to recover from emotional confrontations with Shae, yet here I am, trying to keep my imagination from running away to Aspen and this Christmas and future Christmases and what it would be like to be part of a family like the Giordanis. Thank God Toni can't read my mind, though with the cute little smile on her face and our crazy long eye contact, maybe she can.

Would that be so bad?

Toni opens her mouth to speak but Greta interrupts us. She leans across the table to be heard over the noisy bar. "Let's go tonight. To Aspen."

"What?" I say.

Willa leans across the table. "Greta's going tonight and said we should come, too. We don't have anything going on and kicking my feet up next to a fire pit by a creek drinking a hot toddy sounds pretty good right now."

"Done," Toni says.

"Wait, wait, wait. Hang on," I say and immediately go into panic mode. "I have a list of things I need to do that I've put off, presents to buy—"

"You buy presents year-round," Willa says. "It'll be fine. Let's go!"

"We can go shopping on Sunday in town," Greta says.

I grimace, thinking about how much it would cost to go Christmas shopping in Aspen. It's not that I can't afford it, but old habits die hard.

"We'll go off the beaten path," Toni says.

"Three out of four. You're outvoted," says Willa.

"But, we didn't get to sing karaoke," I say, a little dejected. "Another drink and I would have done my best Mariah Carey."

Willa and Greta both roll their eyes, before putting their empty drinks on the table and making to leave. It seems the decision has been made. I sigh, my shoulders sagging. I prefer to be much more prepared.

As we follow them out of the club, Toni brushes my arm and leans in.

"Don't worry. I'll make sure you get your diva moment in Aspen."

"There's a place to do karaoke?"

"It's a ski town. There're all sorts of trouble we can get up to."

Toni wiggles her eyebrows and I can't help but laugh, and wonder what kind of trouble she has in mind.

CHAPTER NINETEEN
AUDREY

I wake up to the smell of fresh-brewed coffee and an empty side of the bed where my sister should be. She *never* wakes up before I do, especially on the weekends. With her being as bright-eyed and wired as she and Greta were when we arrived at three in the morning, it wouldn't surprise me if Willa didn't get any sleep at all.

I get ready and make myself presentable, but not too presentable. A full face of makeup would be trying too hard, and no one will care anyway.

Last night when we arrived Ingrid and Piero were asleep, and the inside was dark so I couldn't tell much about the house, though the sound of running water sang me to sleep. This morning I'm having trouble picking my jaw up off the floor. The entire back wall is floor-to-ceiling windows looking out on a deck that's built on stilts over a shallow, rock-strewn river. A grove of aspens towers over everything, their leaves shimmering silver in the breeze. The inside is lovingly lived-in, with organized piles of the detritus of life on the counter, forgotten slippers between the coffee table and couch. Family photos on almost every available surface, wall and table. Frayed blankets folded over the backs of chairs. A basket of knitting next to a recliner. A huge orange tabby cat sleeps on the top of a well-worn leather couch. Something delicious bakes in the oven. Bacon, if I'm not mistaken.

I'm surprised to find the kitchen deserted. I expected everyone to be down here drinking coffee and visiting. A normal weekend morning in a cabin in the mountains. Instead I see a coffee mug next to the coffee pot, no doubt left for me by Toni. I smile as I pour coffee into the mug. It is delicious, rich and dark, with just a hint of chocolate. There's nothing better than a good cup of coffee on a chilly morning with the smell of bacon in the oven. Then I notice the coffee cake cooling on the counter.

I could definitely get used to this.

I pause for a moment, looking around once more, and see a few holiday decorations here and there: a Santa in a chef's toque with a mixing bowl and wooden spoon in his hand in the kitchen; a set of three wooden carved wisemen and an angel with pressed-tin silver wings are on the mantel surrounded by fresh boughs of pine; a Santa with a big belly full of Hershey's Kisses; a red-and-green crocheted quilt is thrown over a leather club chair with a very well-worn seat cushion. I can't imagine growing up in a house like this, having a warm, inviting and loving place to go home to. I sigh and almost jump when I feel arms go around my waist and a chin rest on my shoulder. Willa.

"I can't believe people actually live like this," Willa says.

"In a multimillion-dollar house on a river in Aspen?" I tease.

"Well, that, too. Turns out they built this house decades ago before Aspen became 'Aspen.' Piero designed it. Anyway, I came to find you. We're all outside."

She leads me out to the deck where everyone is sitting around a fire pit, drinking coffee and laughing. The snow-covered ground and trees contrast with the warmth of the flames. Willa sits next to Greta, and there's an open chair next to Toni.

Toni's eyes light up when she sees me. She's wearing the same Chris Evans fisherman's sweater she wore to dinner at our house. Her hair is up in a messy bun, tendrils of dark curls escaping around her face and at the nape of her neck, and her face is bare and natural. Toni is relaxed, happy, and absolutely gorgeous. When she sees me, her smile widens. Somehow, her eyes are more electric and stunning here than I've ever seen them in Denver. She very subtly takes me in from head to toe and the thrum of desire that has been humming through my veins since yesterday explodes inside me.

These are going to be the longest four days of my life.

"I found sleepyhead," Willa says.

"It's only seven thirty," I say. "That's hardly sleeping in."

"Leave her alone, Wills," Toni says. "Here, come sit by me."

"Wills?" I say.

"Toni's decided to give me the Prince of Wales' nickname," Willa says.

"Is Willa being high maintenance?" I ask.

"No, she's the perfect guest," Greta says.

Ingrid and Piero stand and turn to me and I feel instantly at ease. I've never been into hippy-dippy stuff, unless you count smoking the occasional joint, but these two have an aura of peace around them that I can almost see. There is nothing but love in their body language and they have a connection and an ease with each other I've rarely seen, and that I envy. I've never had that kind of connection, I've never *seen* that kind of connection, and I want it. I glance at Toni and wonder if I've found that with her. Then inwardly blanch as soon as I think it. I'm not ready for thoughts of a future.

"We're so glad you came," Ingrid says.

"Sorry we showed up early and unannounced," I say.

"Please," Ingrid says. "Greta texted me as soon as you

decided to come last night. We're sorry we didn't wait up, but we have a schedule we like to keep to."

"That's what happens when you get old and set in your ways," Piero says. "Please, sit, sit." Piero waits to sit down until I do.

"I like that sweater," I say to Toni.

Toni grins. "I remember." Our eyes meet and there's so much heat between us I'm glad I can blame my burning cheeks on the fire.

"Audrey, we've been talking about the foundation," Ingrid says. "It was your idea?"

"I suppose technically, but it's all because of Toni's dreams for her division."

"Already making changes to my department, huh?" Piero says good-naturedly. Everyone laughs, and he continues, "No, no, I knew you'd hit the ground running, Toni. Just like you always have."

"I'm starting to wonder if my eyes weren't too big for my stomach," Toni says. "There's so much to do that I feel paralyzed most of the time."

"That's why you make lists," I say. "Set short-term goals of easy tasks. Accomplish something, tick it off the list, move on to the next item."

"This is a woman after my own heart," Ingrid says.

"Mom is the queen of list making," Toni explains.

"No work talk," Willa says. "Let's talk chopping down a Christmas tree. I hear I'm going to have to wrestle you for the ax, Piero."

"Nope, no wrestling. You can have it."

"What?" Toni and Greta say in unison.

"You've never let us touch the ax," Greta says.

"Play your cards right and I'll let you touch my ax," Willa says.

Everyone goes quiet for a beat, then explodes into laughter.

Willa realizes why and says with a red face, "That came out much more suggestive than I meant it to."

"On that note, I think it's time for breakfast," Greta says, to everyone's general agreement.

"I'm going to sit here for a bit and finish my coffee," I say.

"I'll stay with you," Toni offers.

"We'll bring you some food," Willa says.

When everyone is inside I say, "Alone at last."

"For about five minutes, if we're lucky."

"What if I want more than five minutes?" I say. Toni raises her eyebrows, and I laugh. "That came out more suggestive than I meant it to."

"Seems to run in the family," Toni says. She stands, zips up her coat, and says, "Come on. I know just the place."

Our boots crunch through the fresh snow along a thin, winding trail that hugs the bank of the creek running behind the house. We come to a cute little bridge, its rails piled with snow that fell overnight. The creek gurgles beneath us and a bird takes off from a nearby tree, sending a shower of snow onto the ground. A clear blue sky peeks through the trees.

"It's going to be a nice day," Toni says.

She's looking up, giving me a chance to take her in. Her hands are shoved deep into her Fourteener blue down coat, and she's wearing the hiking pants I like so much, because of course she is. Unruly strands of her curly hair stick out from her braid, dark and stark against the snowy landscape, and her blue eyes somehow more vivid in this light than they've ever been before. My stomach swoops as if I'm at the top of a rollercoaster staring down at the long drop, terrified and excited in equal measure.

"Beautiful," I say, my eyes on Toni.

She drops her gaze to me, realizes what I meant, and blushes.

I take a deep breath. "I'm sorry about yesterday. How I snapped at you about Shae. It was completely uncalled for."

"No, no, it's OK," Toni says.

"No, it's not. You didn't say anything I haven't heard from my therapist and Willa. I don't always react well when they say it, either. It's difficult for me to hear because it's true. I know it's true, but I hate that it is. I hate that I turned into a person who would allow herself to be treated like that."

Toni moves close and takes my hands. "Hey, that's not your fault. That's all on Shae. I've watched friends in bad relationships before. They never start bad. It usually happens so gradually you're too deep before you realize."

"I didn't really understand how different I was when I was with Shae until Willa told me last night that she was glad to have her sister back." Toni smiles softly at me and squeezes my hands. I swallow the emotion in my throat. "I wish I could say I didn't know what she meant, but I do. I feel more like myself than I have in a long, long time."

"That's great, Audrey."

"Yeah, it is." I can't help it; my gaze goes to Toni's lips, before finding her beautiful eyes again. "I like you, Toni. A lot. What you said yesterday, about giving me space and time, made me like you even more. Everything about how you handled yesterday made me..." *Want to fuck you senseless*, I think. "... realize that..."

God, how do I say this to her without revealing too much?

I exhale. "What I told you the night we were together is still true. I'm not ready for a serious relationship."

"Sure, of course. Like I said yesterday—"

"But I am ready to have fun now, take things slow, and see what happens."

Toni's mouth falls open a little. She dips her chin and looks at me skeptically. "Are you absolutely sure? Because I can wait. You're worth it."

Christ, could this woman be any more charming?

"I can't," I say, grasping her jacket and pulling her to me.

The hunger I felt for her yesterday, and have been trying like hell to suppress for weeks, flares inside me again. I can't pull her close enough, kiss her deep enough.

We have too many clothes on for me to feel the contours of her body like I want to. I unzip my jacket, then hers, and press our chests together, remembering how her hardened nipples felt against mine that night, her moans when I took her breast in my mouth.

"Oh my God," Toni breathes into my mouth between kisses. She slides a leg between mine and pulls me close. "You kiss me, and all my resolve goes out the window."

She pushes me against the bridge railing and kisses me. Snow plops into the river below; a tree branch creaks in the distance. I grind against Toni's leg, the seam in the crotch of my jeans pressing against my clit. I groan.

My hands find her hair. "Oh my God I love your hair. And this sweater." I slide a hand up her sweater and capture her naked breast in my hand. I pull back. "No bra?"

"A very happy coincidence."

"I'll say." I run my thumb over her hardened nipple. How am I supposed to be strong for the next three days when the feel of Toni's smooth skin and breast in my hand brings back so many wonderful memories? I am so turned on right now that the slightest touch of Toni's would make me come. I'm half tempted to unzip my pants and direct her hand where I'm desperate for it to go, but I don't. I can't. "You are incredibly sexy and naughty and you absolutely bring that out in me."

"Does that mean you'll come to my room tonight?" Toni says, her voice husky with desire.

Oh my God I want this woman so much. "OK, when I say have fun now, I didn't mean this weekend. In the same house as your parents and Greta."

Toni's lips are on my neck. "Don't tell me you've never had sex with the threat you might be heard or get caught."

"Maybe, but not by your sister or your parents." I put my forehead against Toni's. All I want to think about is her breast in my hand, her pebbled nipple against my palm. Her gasps. The crisp air that smells like pine and wood smoke. The sound of the creek trickling over stones beneath the bridge. A far-off woosh of snow falling from a tree. "This moment is perfect," I say.

"You're perfect," Toni whispers.

My instinct is to deflect, to disagree. Instead, I let the compliment sit for a moment. When I decide what to say, we hear Greta yelling at us to come eat.

Toni and I sigh. I remove my hand from beneath her sweater and zip up her coat, while she zips mine.

"Maybe," I say.

"Maybe you're perfect?" Toni teases.

"Oh, no. I'm perfect. And if you play your cards right, *maybe* I'll come to your room tonight."

I know it's not a good idea, but I crave the intimacy we had that night, lying next to each other, hands barely touching, and talking. I hadn't had that with Shae in a long time, maybe never. Vulnerability isn't her strong suit. Hell, it's not typically mine, either. But Toni isn't afraid to put herself out there and tell me exactly what she wants. She thinks I'm worth waiting for. She's amazing, and I want to show her how much I want her.

The happy smile on Toni's face is a sight to behold. I grab her hand and pull her along back toward the house. I stop at the edge of the creek. I bend down and pick up a small gray rock with a white line slashed diagonally through it. I hold it in the palm of my hand and turn it over. It's cold and wet and smooth.

"I'm not punching a hole through that," Toni says.

I push my mouth out in a small pout.

"Oh my God, fine," she says as if it's the biggest imposition in the world, though happiness is written all over her face.

CHAPTER TWENTY

TONI

"I never thought I'd watch my husband and oldest daughter flirt with the same woman," Mom muses.

We sip our mulled wine and watch Audrey, Willa, Greta, and Dad decorate the tree it took us two hours to find. It normally takes us about twenty minutes. Years of tree picking has taught us that unless it's a Charlie Brown tree, you can hide any sort of hole with the back wall, lights, and a few of my pinecone ornaments. Willa and Audrey were determined to find the perfect tree for the house and were just as determined to pay for it as a thank you for including them in the holidays. To my surprise, Dad agreed, but not until he'd argued with them a fair bit. When he saw their enthusiasm for something that we'd long taken for granted, and saw how happy the search made them, he relented.

Now it's cold and snowing outside, there's a huge fire in the hearth, Mom's creamy chicken lasagna is in the oven, I'm sitting on the sofa with Mom, drinking mulled wine, and watching my entire family fall in love with the Adams sisters. My dad is especially taken with Willa and her upbeat personality. My mom is drawn to Audrey's quiet confidence and her occasional silly side. The five of them have been talking about the new foundation for most of the day. It's turning into a Big Deal.

"Audrey and I noticed the flirting a couple of weeks ago. Greta and Willa. I almost chalked it up to two super lesbians assuming everyone else is secretly a lesbian," I say.

Mom chuckles. "I haven't seen Greta ever this relaxed around anyone. The way she lets Willa tease her is something else."

"I know, right? She barely smiles and that somehow eggs on Willa even more."

"Greta wouldn't be nearly as good at flirting with her if she was trying."

"Well, I'm not about to even hint at it because she'll clam up. I really like this version of her."

Mom looks at me. "She's always been there, Toni. You just couldn't see past your jealousy."

It hurts, a little, hearing that truth so brutally relayed by my mom. But, she's not wrong. "I know."

Mom's eyes widen and her brows rise. "What?"

"You're right. Though I'm not sure jealousy is the word. I just always wanted her to notice me. To appreciate me. She never did, so I acted like a brat to her and about her."

"Well, Greta's like me. We're better at being critical than complimentary, but that doesn't mean we don't talk behind your back about how wonderful you are."

I give my mom a sidelong look and, sure enough, she's joking. I play along, though, because there is probably more truth in it than she's willing to admit. "It would be nice if you would say it to my face."

"From what I hear, Greta has," Mom says.

"So, you do talk about me behind my back," I bristle.

"We talk business behind your back. But that's going to change from now on. You'll be part of the conversation. She told you how critical your plans are."

"Yeah, about that." I hesitate. There's something to be said about putting words out in the world and making them manifest. If I put my fears out on the table, will they consume me? Will it put a chink in the facade of confidence I've spent years building? I inhale deeply and say, "I'm not sure I'm up for it."

Mom studies me with her clear blue eyes that are so much like mine. "Why?"

"I'm not the type of person who has five- and ten-year plans."

"Doesn't mean you can't have them."

"It's just all so different from before. I really liked my life."

"I know you did. We funded it. You needed a change."

"Did I?" I ask, skepticism dripping from my voice.

"Let me put this another way," Mom says. "You've never had to work for anything in your life. It's time you did. For what it's worth, Greta's not the only one at the office that's bragged on the job you're doing, you know. What's brought all this on?"

Shae's bullshit comment. I shrug. "I see how much work all my big ideas need and how long it will all take, I'm just not sure I'm up for being out of the field for that much and that long."

Mom nods. "You aren't going to be stuck in the office. Aren't you going to New Zealand in a couple of weeks for business?"

"Yes."

"Figure out your limit of office time and schedule trips before you reach the end of your rope. Give the office a year, OK?"

"A year?" My palms start sweating at the mere idea of being inside for a year.

"It'll go by faster than you think."

I finally hear something she said moments ago. "Other people have said I'm doing a good job?" I ask, hating how hopeful and needy my voice sounds.

Mom smiles at me. "Yes, and I'm not surprised one bit. I

knew putting you in charge was the right decision. I'm very proud of you," Mom says quietly.

I can't help my little yelp of astonishment. Mom never compliments me. "Wha... how did you... what in the world made you think I could do this?"

"You like to exude this whole air of chill mountain woman, but no one can be as good as you are at what you do without being careful and diligent and completely focused." She looks at me full on, with the same half-smile that Greta does so well. "You're more like me, and Greta, than you want to admit."

I turn away quickly so she doesn't see the tears that well in my eyes. I'm not sure why I'm crying. Is it because I've somehow managed to get Greta and Mom's approval, or is the idea that I'm anything like them so horrifying it makes me want to weep. I need to talk to Audrey about this.

That stops me. It's the first time I've thought of her first in an emotionally charged situation that didn't involve her, but as soon as the initial shock is over, I know that it's absolutely right. She's who I want to talk to for her advice, her feedback. To watch as she listens to me, her face a study in focus and concentration on me, and only me, and my problem, as if it's the most important thing in the world to her.

As if I'm the most important thing in the world to her.

I'm staring at Audrey while I think all of this. She catches me staring and smiles, then pulls a dorky face. I laugh.

"She's good for you," Mom says.

"Yeah. Greta said that last night."

"You're welcome."

"Oh, so you're the reason Greta is suddenly so zen about me and Audrey?"

Mom shrugs one shoulder. "Well, I didn't hurt the situation." Mom sips her mulled wine. "Your dad and I approve."

A huge grin spreads across my face. "She's great, isn't she?"

"She is. She reminds me of your sister."

"What? No way. Gross, Mom."

Mom laughs outright at that. The oven beeps and she gets up to take out the lasagna.

"We're out of ornaments," Audrey says.

"That means it's done," Willa says. "I'm out of wine."

"I'll get you some," Greta says.

"Allow me," Dad says, at the same time.

Audrey comes over and sits next to me. She's glowing with happiness. "I'm having such a great time."

"I'm glad," I say. "I think my parents like you and Willa more than me and Greta."

"Speak for yourself," Greta says.

"Of course they do," Willa says, taking a glass of wine from Greta. "We're awesome, aren't we, Audrey?"

"So I've been told."

"Dinner's ready," Dad says.

I stand from the couch and hold my hand out to Audrey, whose gaze is raking over my body. When her eyes meet mine, her mouth has quirked into a sexy half-smile. She stands, puts her soft cheek against mine and whispers in my ear, "You are wearing too many clothes," sending a shudder through my body.

She pulls away with a cocky, mischievous expression on her beautiful face.

"Tease."

"One hundred percent," she says, before turning and heading to the kitchen.

"The tree looks amazing," I say to Dad.

"It hasn't looked this good in years," he agrees.

"I think that's a thinly veiled insult directed at us, Greta," I say.

Greta carries the lasagna to the table. "No, that insult was pretty direct." She laughs.

"Oh my God that smells delicious," Audrey says.

"It's definitely not tuna casserole," Willa says.

After a flurry of getting everything on the table, Mom directing everyone where to sit, and pouring wine, we all raise our glasses in a toast. My dad, the sentimental one, says, "To our wonderful new friends. Thank you for sharing the holidays with us. I know I speak for Ingrid, Greta, and Antonia when I say we hope that you come back soon and often."

We all clink glasses and drink. I catch Audrey's eyes over the rim of the glass and wink.

She smiles and raises her glass again. "To the Giordanis. Thank you for welcoming us into your home, and into your family. I can speak for Willa and me: this is the best holiday we've ever had."

"So far," Willa says.

"Who knows? It might all go downhill from here," I tease, and everyone laughs.

CHAPTER TWENTY-ONE

TONI

"I'd forgotten how insufferable you are when you're drunk."

It's after midnight and Mom and Dad have gone to sleep. The four of us are sitting in front of the fireplace, in various states of sobriety, meaning Audrey and I are sober, and Willa and Greta are drunk.

"I'm not drunk," Greta says.

"The ice queen has melted," Willa says before cracking up laughing.

"Maybe a little," says Greta. She turns my way. "You've been telling me to loosen up for years. Here I am, loosened up, all for you, Tiny Dancer."

"Do *not* call me that," I say.

"Oh my God your name does sound like Tiny Dancer," Audrey says.

"Please don't encourage them," I say.

"I love that song." Willa sighs, before singing at the top of her lungs, and out of tune.

I grimace.

Audrey chuckles. She leans in close. "Yeah, Willa can't sing sober, either."

"You're singing it wrong," Greta says and, as I knew she would, she breaks into the song I hate more than any other on the planet. Well, her special version of the song. "Hold me closer, Toni Danzig! Count the pimples on your forehead! Belay me down a big old rock face. You had your coming out today!"

"Come on." I don't particularly want Audrey to hear about days as a baby gay, which Greta has helpfully chronicled with more and more stanzas of that fucking song over the years.

But Greta keeps going. "Handsome dy-y-ke/riding her bi-i-ke/handing rainbows out for Pride/Baby gay/With big wide eyes/Lost it to a butch named Rae..."

"You've got a great voice, Great," Willa says. "Wait, I mean Greta."

"No, that's fine," Greta says. "I'll answer to Great."

Willa stands up. "Well, come on, Great. Show me these stars you were talking about at our place that night. I expect to be wowed."

Greta stands and she's surprisingly sure-footed for someone who is supposedly drunk. I wonder if Greta isn't playing it up so she can have an excuse tomorrow morning for having so much fun tonight.

"Let's get bundled up," Greta says.

"Oh, we'll be fine."

"No, we won't." She steers Willa into the mud room and closes the door behind them. Audrey and I sit in silence and listen to the two of them banter and flirt and gently argue as they get dressed for the weather. We laugh at Willa's controlled chaos, and at Greta's somehow enduring patience. Finally, they're out the door and we are left with only the sound of the fire crackling.

"Are they going to be OK?" Audrey asks.

"Greta's in charge, so absolutely."

"I don't think Willa's as drunk as she's putting on."

"Funny, I thought the same about Greta."

We give each other knowing looks, then die laughing.

"Tiny Dancer, huh?" Audrey says.

"I really hate that song."

"It's not my favorite Elton John song, either."

We're sitting on the couch, far enough away to be safe while others were in the room. Now, Audrey moves closer.

"Is there anything I can do to get that scowl off your face?" Her tongue traces her lips and her gaze glides up and down my body.

"I'm not sure. It's put me in a pretty bad mood."

"Hmm." She stands and swings her leg over mine to straddle my lap. My hands automatically go to her hips. "Does this help?"

"A little." I pull her hips toward me, bring her center flush against me. "Getting better."

She cups my jaw and pulls me to her. I think she's going to kiss me, but her lips go to my neck, her breath in my ear. "I promised myself I would be strong and not do this."

"Why would you do a silly thing like that?" I ask.

"I'm having a very hard time remembering right now. Being around you all day has weakened my resolve." I push my hips up and into her. Her breath catches and she lets out a small groan. "I love the way you smell."

There's my desire, revived with one whisper. "Oh my God," I whimper.

A month ago, I would have flipped any woman who said that to me onto the couch and fucked them senseless. But this is Audrey.

This is Audrey.

My better angels take over (I didn't realize I had them, either) and I push her away slightly. "Are you sure about this?"

She sits back onto my thighs. "Toni, we're having sex, not renting a U-Haul."

"Right. I know."

"Are you sure you're OK with that?"

I sit up straight and slide my hand behind her head, bringing her lips closer to mine, and look into her eyes. "Audrey, I've wanted you every second of every day since you walked out the door that night."

Audrey inhales softly, and her eyes darken. "So have I."

"I'll take you however I can get you."

I stand up, keeping Audrey in my arms. She wraps her legs around my waist and grins. I walk toward the stairs.

"Putting those forearms to good use finally," she teases.

"I'm thankful for every arm day I've had at the gym."

I stop at the foot of the stairs and kiss her, long and hard. Audrey groans deep within her throat. I pull my lips away from hers.

"But I think carrying you up the stairs and kissing you while I do it is beyond even my skills." I drop Audrey onto the floor, grab her hand, and pull her up the stairs to my room.

The door is barely closed and locked behind us before I'm on her, cupping her face. There is no way in hell I'm going to let the moment I've been waiting for for weeks slip out of my grasp by overthinking things.

"Your lips are just as perfect as I remember." I pour all the emotions I can't say—I *shouldn't* say—into our kiss. It's gentle and slow, and we immediately start shedding our clothes, our lips parting only to toss them aside. Then we are on the bed and Audrey is beneath me and I settle down on top of her. My body sings at the feel of her soft curves and her satiny skin. She slides her hands down my side and to my ass. She purrs.

"I have wanted to get my hands on your ass for weeks. Could you tell?"

"I had a pretty good idea. I've caught you staring a few times."

"I know. But you keep wearing the gray pants."

"Gee, I wonder why."

"It's a real mystery," Audrey replies.

We're both grinning.

"Tell me what you want," I say.

"I want your mouth on me."

"Where?"

"Everywhere."

"This may take a while," I say.

"The longer the better."

"Challenge accepted."

I place the first kiss on her forehead and trace her face with my lips. Then I trace her jaw with my tongue on my way to kissing and nibbling her long neck. Audrey's hands are in my hair, and she cranes her neck to give me all the access I need to kiss every inch. I feel a moan vibrate in her throat, her pulse beat quickly in the soft hollow below her ear. I inhale deeply, the scent that has been tantalizing me at the most inopportune times: standing next to Audrey in the break room, sitting in her desk chair to leave a note and smelling her perfume that lingers on her vest she has draped over the chair back.

"Hmm, your mouth feels wonderful," she purrs. "Bite my collarbone. Gently."

I obey. She flinches slightly and her moan sends a surge of desire through me. It is such a turn-on to make love to a woman who knows what she wants and is confident enough to ask for it. I lift my head and our gazes meet. Her fingers are entangled in my hair and she's massaging my head softly. "Tell me more," I say.

"I want to see your dark hair fanned out across my pale skin while your tongue and mouth destroy me." She quirks an eyebrow. "Over and over."

"Fuck me, you are so sexy."

She arranges my hair across her chest while I kiss my way down her stomach to settle between her legs. She moans and lifts her hips in encouragement. I kiss both inner thighs and pause, before touching the tip of my tongue to Audrey's clit and pulling back. She makes a little noise, and I do it again, a little more contact, for a split second longer. I continue to tease her with touches and small, almost imperceptible licks on only her clit. Her frustration finally gets the best of her and she groans loudly.

"Tease," she says. "Don't stop."

"Never," I say.

Our gazes meet and her mouth turns up into the sexiest grin I've ever seen. "Promises, promises," she says.

For the next hour, I tease her with my mouth, tongue, fingers, and a small bullet vibe I tossed in my duffle with hope in my heart.

I take her to the edge four times, and bring her down, until she is whimpering my name and begging me to destroy her. I am on the edge myself, desperate for my own release.

I flip on my back and pull her on top of me. She straddles me, and the sight of her, flushed with desire, her nipples hard, is the most gorgeous goddamn sight I've ever seen.

I slide three fingers inside her and am going to press the vibe against her when she stops me.

"Come with me," she says, her voice ragged and hoarse. She presses my hand, and the vibe, against my swollen clit.

I buck against her, my orgasm coursing through my veins like a tidal wave. Audrey clamps a hand over her mouth, but can't restrain a long, low whine as she clenches around my fingers and drenches the palm of my hand, and shudders her release.

CHAPTER TWENTY-TWO

TONI

My family has always lived by the early to rise early to bed ethos and even though I got very little sleep last night, I'm wide awake at five thirty in the morning. I watch Audrey sleep next to me, her eyes moving back and forth beneath her lids. She's dreaming about something. I hope it's good.

I consider waking her. The pull to taste her again, to feel her hot and wet against my mouth, to hear her moan my name when my tongue lazily circles her clit, and her hiss of breath when I slide my fingers inside her, is almost impossible to resist. I suspected before but last night confirmed it; I will always want more of Audrey Adams.

My better angels win, again, and I don't wake her. I don't want to disturb her REM sleep.

When we had finally collapsed an hour or so ago from exhaustion, she mentioned how sore she would be in the morning.

"I'm sorry," I said, though I wasn't really.

"No, you're not," she said with a lazy, sated smile. "I'm not either. It is a very good kind of sore. Our little secret." She kissed me on the cheek and rolled over, pressed her leg next to mine so we were still touching, and fell asleep almost immediately. So, she's not a post-sex snuggler. I guess she can't be perfect.

I fell asleep within two minutes, like usual, slept hard, and woke up at five thirty on the dot.

Our little secret.

I dress with those words running through my mind on a loop. No matter how I turn them around, front to back, back to front, the meaning is pretty clear.

Audrey wants to keep *us* a secret.

Fun for now, seeing where things go, I'm OK with that. Well, mostly OK. But keeping it a secret?

I stand at the door to the room, one hand on the doorknob, my gaze on Audrey's sleeping form. Wake her up and get a little clarity? Or let her sleep and read the subtext?

We're having sex, Toni. Not renting a U-Haul.

Is this what taking it slow means for Audrey? Keeping us a secret? Because that's not what it means to me. That's not what I want.

I should be OK with casual; I've done casual for a decade. But I've never done casual in secret. It seems like an unnecessary complication to an already complicated situation—working together, her getting out of a toxic relationship, me learning how to navigate being in a relationship, in whatever form this might take.

Yeah, I might have failed to mention that I've never been in a serious relationship. Luckily, I know someone nearby who has, and will be free with advice.

"Hey."

I jump at the sound of Audrey's sleepy voice. "Hey, there. I didn't want to wake you."

She rubs her eyes and squints at me through the dark. "Are you OK? You've been standing there staring into space for a while."

"Yeah, I'm good. Go back to sleep."

"What time is it?"

"Five thirty."

"I should probably go to my room."

"My family is probably all awake and downstairs so you shouldn't get caught sneaking next door."

She smiles. "OK."

Just talk to her, you idiot.

Instead, I say, "I'm going to go snowshoeing."

"Oh my God you're a morning person."

I laugh. "I guess you aren't."

"Very reluctantly and only because I read in a self-help book once that all successful executives get up at three a.m."

"I'm not *that* much of a morning person."

"Thank God." She smiles sleepily at me. "You're beautiful. Have I ever told you that?"

My heart swells. "Not in so many words. I think you said, 'you're sexy as fuck' when I finger fucked you last night."

"Hmm, I remember," she says. "Tonight, it's my turn."

"You might want to recharge the little vibe," I say. "Cord is in the drawer."

"Yes, we haven't talked about your foresight on bringing a vibe, or is it your travel vibe?"

"I bought a brand-new one just for you," I say.

Audrey raises her eyebrows. She throws the blankets back and rises from the bed, all smooth creamy skin, long legs, and full, beautiful breasts. Shit, why didn't I wake her up?

"And you got lavender, my favorite color," she says in a teasing voice.

"Happy coincidence."

"Can I give you a kiss goodbye?"

"I'm afraid if I kiss you or touch you I won't let you leave this room all day."

"We'll have to be strong," she whispers, her mouth almost touching mine.

"I can be strong," I say. Then I step back, open the door and go through quickly. I peek back in through the crack. The shock on Audrey's face is totally worth it.

"Weren't expecting that, were you?" I say with a grin. "Go back to sleep, lazybones. Coffee'll be hot when you get up."

I close the door, leaving Audrey shocked and, hopefully, very turned on.

Greta stands in the kitchen, holding a mug of coffee, staring into space.

"Hey," I say.

She startles, then tries to act natural. "Good morning. Sleep well?"

"Like a rock. You?"

Greta turns to me full on and I'm shocked by how tired she looks. The skin around her eyes has been caked with concealer, but dark circles still manage to peek through.

"Yeah. Like a rock," she says.

We're both lying, and we both know it.

"Was Willa impressed with the stars?"

"Yes," Greta says, coolly. She deliberately holds my gaze, daring me to probe.

I'm not an idiot. I keep my mouth shut. Besides, she'll reject any attempt I make to get her to open up—God forbid she acknowledge that I could help her with something—and right now I need advice she can't help me with.

"I'm going to go snowshoeing," I say. "Back in a bit."

"Have fun," she deadpans, and walks out of the kitchen and up the stairs.

In ten minutes, I'm kitted up and out on the trail. In twenty, I'm using the spare key to unlock the basement door of Max's parents' house. I shed all my gear, sneak into Max's room, and climb into bed with her like I've done hundreds of times in our lives.

Max sleeps on her side in a fetal position and I mirror it and watch her. With her eyes closed she says, "You're kidding me right now."

"Nope."

She sighs and opens her eyes. "What the fuck are you doing sneaking into my bed on Christmas Eve."

"Oh, shit. I forgot it was Christmas Eve."

"Would that have mattered?"

"Nope. I need your help."

"Obviously." Max rolls on her back and rubs her face. "You know one day I'm going to call in all these favors and you're going to sorely regret this."

"Looking forward to it."

She drops her hand and looks at me. "Oh no, I'm going to make you miserable, Tone."

"And I'm sure I will deserve every needle you poke into my voodoo doll. Are you done pretending to not want to help me?"

"If it helps me get back to sleep sooner, yes. What's up?"

"I slept with Audrey."

"Yes, I know. In my bed."

"No. A few hours ago. In my bed."

Max throws up her hands. "And? Did you come here to brag about getting laid?"

"I don't do that."

She sighs. "I don't even have the energy. You talk, I'll listen. Go."

I fill her in as quickly and succinctly as possible.

"So, you think she's sending you mixed signals," Max says.

"Maybe? Or maybe not. She doesn't want to rush into a relationship, but she wants to have sex, but she wants to keep it a secret. Are those mixed signals or all kinda the same?"

"And instead of talking to her when you had the chance, you decided to wake me up and ask me to read her mind. Sounds about right."

"Well, when you put it like that," I say. I lie back on the bed and stare at the ceiling. "I've never been in a relationship and you have so I thought you'd know what I should do."

"Toni, I've been in five relationships in ten years. That's hardly a good track record for giving advice."

"Who else am I going to talk to? Greta? I don't think she's been on a date since she went to work at the company."

"Audrey. You should have talked to Audrey."

"I don't want to be the one who's always, *Hey let's have a deep conversation about our pseudo relationship*, because I could absolutely go there very easily. We'd just had amazing sex. I didn't want to ruin it."

"You mean you don't want to jeopardize tonight's great sex."

God, I hate it when Max reads me so easily. "Fuck you," I say. "I want more than she does, I know that."

"Were you lying when you said you'd take it slow?"

"No, of course not. But I don't think keeping it a secret from our family—"

"Your family."

"—my family, means we're rushing things."

"You know what solves all these problems? Communication."

"So, you're saying I should talk to her."

"Yes, Toni. Jesus, I can't believe you woke me up for this. Go away."

"You don't want to snuggle?"

"Go snuggle with Audrey."

"She's not a snuggler."

"That's a you problem, not a me problem."

"You aren't very helpful."

"Danzig, payback is going to be hell for this one."

I get up from the bed and make it to the door when Max sits up and says, "Wait."

I leap onto the bed and tackle her. "You want to snuggle. I knew it."

"No, I don't," she protests, but she lets me pull her down onto the bed and snuggle up to her side.

"OK, keep protesting," I say. "Your secret is safe with me," I whisper.

Max sighs, but I feel her relax. It must be exhausting to be deadpan and cynical all the time.

"Audrey is trying to set boundaries, but not doing a great job of it," Max says. "You need her to define taking it slow. For her. Then you need to tell her what taking it slow is for you. Just because she's getting out of a bad relationship doesn't mean you have to just agree to everything she wants. She wants to take it slow. But you don't want to keep it a secret. Seems like a fair trade. Just don't go agreeing to everything she wants because you're afraid you're going to lose her."

"You give good advice," I say.

"Too bad you rarely take it."

"Not true."

"Speaking of advice, how's the apartment search going?"

"I'm going to, I promise. I've been really busy and I'm about to take a couple of trips and be gone for weeks and it seems silly to get a place that will immediately stand empty."

Max sighs. "Just say you hate apartment hunting."

"I hate apartment hunting."

"Good thing I don't."

"You've found me an apartment?"

"No, I've found *me* an apartment. You can sub-let mine starting March 1."

"I don't want to kick you out of your place."

"You aren't. I'm ready for something bigger. Newer. That has an elevator."

"Are you sure?"

"If it means I don't have to see your naked ass walking through the house all the time, then yes."

"You love my naked ass and you know it."

"In your dreams." Max turns over. "Now, go away so I can get some sleep."

I hug her from behind. "I love you, Maxine."

"Call me that again and I swear to God no one will ever find your body."

"You need to stop listening to true crime podcasts," I say, and jump out of the bed, feeling lighter than I have in weeks.

"I need them to dull all of the emotional pain and baggage I have from my best friend," she says, her voice muffled by the pillow.

I pause at the door. "I think you're being sarcastic right now, but I can't tell because of the pillow. We'll revisit this one day. Promise. See? Look at me. Wanting to communicate all over the place. Who knew communication was the key?"

"Literally everyone," Max says.

I close the door behind me and walk through the house to leave, saying goodbye to Max's unsurprised parents on the way out.

CHAPTER TWENTY-THREE

AUDREY

Willa is awake and sitting up in bed looking at her phone when I try to sneak into the room we're sharing. She looks at me over the top of her glasses.

"Well, at least it was a short walk of shame."

I chuckle. "No shame here at all," I say.

"That good?"

I let out a slow breath. "Beyond good. Stratospheric."

Willa raises her eyebrows. "So things are going to be weird and awkward today. Got it. Merry Christmas Eve, by the way." She returns her attention to her phone.

"Merry Christmas Eve to you, too." I don't need to have a special mental connection with my twin to see, and feel, that something is wrong.

"Why are you awake?"

"Watching cleaning videos."

"What level cleaning?"

"Hoarders."

Oh no. If she's watching hoarder houses be emptied and cleaned that means she's already been through the power-washing, rug-cleaning, and car-detailing videos. Transformation videos like these calm Willa when something in her life has grown into an unavoidable problem. The bigger the mess cleaned, the bigger her problem.

"What's wrong?" I ask.

"Nothing," she replies.

"What happened?"

She drops her phone, takes off her glasses, and sighs. "You slept with Toni, and now everything is going to be all weird."

"No, it won't."

"You two will either be all lovey-dovey or you'll pretend to ignore each other. Either way, it will be weird and we have six more months of this shit."

"Where is this coming from? I thought you liked Toni."

"I do, but I'm not going to distract Greta so you two can go fuck in the supply closet at work."

"Willa, Jesus. That's not going to happen. One, that's totally unprofessional. Two, Toni and I are just having fun."

Willa's mouth drops open. "Audrey, I know you aren't that stupid. Though maybe you are. Toni's in love with you—and don't look all shocked when I say that, you know it's true. I didn't expect her to be strong enough to give you lots of time, but I really didn't expect you to try to seduce her so soon."

"I didn't seduce her. It was mutual, trust me."

"You're in love with her, too?"

"God, no. I didn't say that. It's way too early for love. Why are you suddenly so against this?"

"The first time I criticize you and you try to turn it back around on me. Maybe you learned a little too much from being with Shae."

"Hey! That's unfair. I'm not turning it back around on you. From the very first day in the office you talked about me bending Toni over a table. I never asked you to distract Greta and I didn't even know for sure that's what you were doing. In fact, you seemed to enjoy it quite a bit."

"This isn't about me and Greta. There is nothing but friendship between me and Greta."

"Are you sure about that? Because it's pretty obvious there is to everyone else."

Willa levels me with a hard stare. "I'm positive."

We glare at each other for a long moment and I debate whether or not I should call her out on her lie. I've seen this expression from Willa before, not often, but I know now is definitely not the time to push her.

"OK," I say.

She visibly relaxes and releases a sharp exhale. She pats the bed next to her, and opens her arms. "Come here."

I lie down next to her and she wraps me up in a hug. "God, you smell like sex."

"Sorry."

"No, you're not. How did you leave it with Toni?"

"Um, I didn't really. She left early to go snowshoeing, of all things."

"After having sex all night?"

"I know. But, last night, before, we agreed to have fun and take things slow."

"She agreed to that?"

"Well, yeah. She said she would take me however she could get me."

"Hmm," Willa says, watching me. "I hope she meant it."

So do I.

I take a shower and then go downstairs to meet Willa for coffee. We aren't the first ones up, of course. Willa is in the kitchen, washing dishes, while Ingrid potters around cooking. Greta is sitting at the kitchen table on her computer, her hair up, and her business face on.

"Merry Christmas Eve," I say.

Everyone greets me, though Greta's eyes don't leave her computer.

I go to her. "Everything OK?"

She looks up, and I realize her eyes were unfocused, not really seeing her computer. "Oh, yeah. Everything's fine."

"Here's some coffee, Auds," Willa says. She puts the mug on the table. "Want a refresh, Greta?"

"No, thank you."

Willa sips her coffee and turns to me. "It's ornament day. Decided what you're going to do?"

"I picked up a rock yesterday and Toni said she'd punch a hole in it for me."

"What do you usually do, Greta?" Willa asks.

"Popcorn garland," she says.

"Sounds good, I'll help," Willa says. "And by help, I mean I'll hold the bowl, eat the popcorn, and watch you."

"It's just plain popcorn," Greta says.

"You don't make festive-colored caramel popcorn?"

"No. I like plain."

Willa nods slowly and sips her coffee. "Well, that tracks," she says, and walks off.

Greta's face flames with embarrassment or anger, I'm not sure which, and I don't have time to think about what just happened because Toni bounds into the house.

When I see her I forget to breathe. I've never seen her look so gorgeous. Her eyes sparkle, her skin is bright with exertion and a little red from the cold, especially her nose. She's smiling and I imagine this is what she always looks like after she's been out hiking or skiing or snowshoeing or whatever crazy shit she does. Her energy fills the house, overpowering everything and everyone, jolting us out of our lethargy. Toni's here. The day is alive with possibility.

"Where have you been?" Willa asks.

"I snowshoed over to Max's place, then did a five-mile loop."

"I'm sorry, did you say five miles?" Willa asks. She's still in her flannel pajamas, with a thick navy sweater thrown over the top. She looks cozy and rather beautiful.

"I did," Toni says.

Her eyes meet mine and blood roars through my body like class-five river rapids in the spring. I'm glad I'm sitting down because there's no way my knees wouldn't have buckled with the force of Toni's charisma and my attraction to her.

She grins and walks toward me, taking off her beanie as she does. Her hair is absolute chaos, sticking out from her head with static electricity from the wool cap. So, I'm distracted when she comes up to me, leans down, says, "Merry Christmas Eve, Audrey," and kisses me on the mouth.

CHAPTER TWENTY-FOUR

TONI

I don't realize my mistake until I pull away from the kiss—a very sweet and tender one, I might add—see the expression on Audrey's face, and realize there is a vacuum of silence in our kitchen.

I have the crazy idea to cover my mistake by kissing Willa, too, and even turn toward her. She obviously reads the panic written all over my face, and somehow has the same idea as me.

"My turn," she says, and steps forward.

"Merry Christmas Eve, Willa," I say, and kiss her as quickly as possible. But she won't let me go and holds me to her for what seems like forever, but is probably only a few seconds, about the length of time I kissed Audrey. Thank God the kiss I gave Audrey was pretty chaste, or I think Willa would go for more.

When she pulls back, she turns to Greta with a big smile and open arms. "Your turn, Greta."

"I've already wished you merry Christmas Eve." Greta's voice is as stiff as her expression.

"Oh right. Last night. I forgot. If you would have added a kiss, like Toni, I'd remember." Willa turns to my mom, whose eyes are wide. "What can I do to help, Ingrid? Dishes are washed. Anything else for your sous chef?"

I appreciate how Willa is trying to brazen this all out, to make it normal so Audrey and I can talk later, but it's definitely not working.

"Um, well," my mom says.

She and Dad glance at each other and Dad says, "Ingrid, remember that thing I, uh, wanted to show you in, erm, the workshop?" If this wasn't the start of a dumpster fire, I would laugh at how comically high my dad's voice goes at the end of the question.

"Yes, absolutely. Let's do that now." And at that my mom, who has never been one to shirk a confrontation, practically sprints out of the kitchen.

Once they're out of the room, and I hear the back door close behind them, I have no choice but to turn around to Audrey. She's sitting in much the same position as I left her. That has to be good, right?

"Audrey, I'm sorry. I wasn't thinking and..." I trail off. No. I'm not going to say what she wants to hear, I'm going to say what I want, what I meant. "It's not a big deal. It's just my family."

"And that is our cue to exit, Greta," Willa says.

She starts towards the stairs, but Greta seems glued to her seat.

Audrey stands. "We'll go."

I follow Audrey up the stairs and to my room, and close the door behind us.

"Look, I'm really sorry, Audrey. When I saw you and you were looking at me like that I just forgot where I was and who else was there. All I thought was how happy I was to see you first thing in the morning, in my childhood home, on my favorite holiday." I move close and pull her to me. "How I hope this is the first of many."

Audrey steps out of my embrace. "OK, stop. This is not taking it slow, Toni."

"Audrey..."

"No. The kiss, I understand." She looks at me. "I wanted to kiss you, too. But all the rest of it. I'm not ready for any of that."

"Which is why we're going to take it slow."

"Kissing me in front of your family is not taking it slow, Toni. Talking about future holidays together is the very opposite of taking it slow."

"I can't want those things?"

Audrey sighs and looks up at the ceiling, as if searching for the answers. Finally she looks me dead in the eye and says, "I don't want those things."

I feel as if I've been punched in the solar plexus. "What?" I say, in a voice strangled with shock.

"I thought I made it pretty clear yesterday that I just want to have fun. Like you offered that first night. No strings. That's the kind of rela— attachments you're used to, right?"

I'm listening to her but barely understand the words coming out of her mouth. Her expression is so far removed from how she looked at me when I came into the house not five minutes ago I wonder which one is real, which expression is a figment of my imagination. They both can't be right.

"I don't want that with you," I manage to say.

"You don't want to have fun?"

"I don't want it to be that... shallow. We aren't that shallow." There's a flicker in her mask, and I know I've hit a nerve. "You felt it that night, too, Audrey. That connection. I didn't imagine it."

"That night was amazing and fun, but there was nothing more."

"Audrey, I fell in lov—"

"No," Audrey says. "You do not get to say that to me right now."

I bristle, and Max's words come back to me. "Oh, I don't get to say that I love you? That I started falling in love with you the moment I saw you in Dewey's that night and have been falling further and further every day since?"

"No! Fuck, Toni. It's too soon."

"You don't get to tell me what I can say or how I can feel, Audrey. All I've done is be respectful of what you've wanted, every step of the way. I was ready to give you all the time you needed after the Christmas party, but you decided that you wanted me. That you were ready. I shouldn't have given in, but I did. You want to take it slow, and I will. But letting my family know that we're seeing each other isn't rushing things. Telling you how I feel isn't rushing things."

"Telling me you've loved me since you set eyes on me is leveling things up pretty far, Toni."

"If I was asking you to marry me, or move in with me, then yeah. But I'm not. I'm not ready for that, either. But, yes, I want that with you long term."

Max's words echo in my head. *There's nothing wrong with asking for what you want, Toni.*

Fuck it.

I inhale. "I love you, Audrey, and I want to grow old with you."

Audrey's head jerks back as if I slapped her, and her eyes go comically wide. Any subliminal hope I'd harbored that my declaration would make her melt into a pile of goo and declare her undying love is shattered when her shocked expression morphs into something like resignation.

"I can't say those words, Toni. Any of them."

"It's OK," I say quickly. "You don't have to. I just wanted you to know how I feel."

"But I *didn't* want to know," Audrey says. "I don't need, or want, that pressure, the responsibility."

"Responsibility? For what?"

"Your feelings. It doesn't matter what I feel, it will never live up to 'I want to grow old with you.' Jesus, Toni, what are you thinking? Laying something like that on me after I've known you a month? Not just me but on anyone? There is nothing about this conversation that goes along with what we agreed to last night. Or did you just agree to whatever would get you laid?"

Now I'm getting angry. "First of all, you came on to me, let's not forget that. Second, it wasn't like we had a huge conversation about any of this."

"We could have if you hadn't left the room so quickly this morning."

She had a point, but I ignored it. "You're blowing this all way out of proportion. We are going to take it slow, I promise. I just wanted you to know how I felt so that..."

Audrey crosses her arms over her chest. "So that what?"

I inhale. I had no idea it would be this fucking hard to ask for what I want, to put myself, if not first, at least on equal standing, with Audrey. "So that you aren't the only one who gets what she wants out of this relationship, which is kind of how it's been so far. You've set all the rules, and I've gone along because I want to be with you. But I'm part of this relationship, too, and you need to get that."

"You're absolutely right. That's what I want in a relationship, too. Eventually. But I can't give that to you right now. I have to put myself first, professionally and personally."

"I understand," I say. "We can—"

"Stop," Audrey says sharply. "Will you please just fucking listen to me?"

"I am."

"No you're not." She closes her eyes and rubs her forehead. "I can't do this again." She looks me in the eye, her expression hard. "Stop trying to charm me into giving in and going along. Grow up, Toni. Take no for an answer. I don't want a relationship with you."

Audrey steps around me, careful to avoid touching me, and leaves the room.

CHAPTER TWENTY-FIVE
AUDREY

"Thank God," I say when I see Willa sitting on our bed, on her phone, in much the same pose as she was a few hours ago. I close the door behind me. "We have to go. Now."

Willa swings her legs off the bed and sits up, ready for action. "Why? What happened?"

I grab my suitcase, plop it on the bed, and start rounding up my stuff. "I just drove a stake through Toni's heart."

"Did she turn into a vampire?"

I huff out a frustrated sigh. "Now is not the time for jokes, Willa."

"It's obviously also not the time for metaphors, Audrey, but that didn't stop you. What. Happened?"

I stop winding the cord to my Mac around the charging block. "She told me she was in love with me and wanted to grow old with me."

"Shit," Willa says softly.

"And I just couldn't, Willa. I couldn't handle it. I'm not ready for that, not anywhere close. Yes, I like Toni, a lot, and who knows what I might feel for her down the line. I mean, is this lust I feel now or something more? But she's like well past the 'let's take it slow and find out' and I tried to tell her and she wouldn't listen and I kept trying and she kept..." I'm shaking so hard the neat bundle I've made of my cord falls apart. "Stupid tiny charging block," I say as I try to rewind it, before it falls out of my hands and into the suitcase.

Willa is around the bed in a flash and holding me close. "Hey, hey, shhh. It's OK. I got ya."

"It felt just like talking to Shae and I knew that if I didn't—if she kept—I had—her expression when I—" I can't talk; I can't breathe. Willa must be hugging me too hard because it feels like something or someone is sitting on my chest.

"OK, sit down," Willa says. "Head between your knees."

She sits next to me, her hand on my back, until my breathing returns to normal. Even then I keep my head on my knees so she won't see the tears in my eyes.

"Stay here," she says. "I'll take care of everything."

Willa leaves the room and I'm alone. I hear another door close in the distance and wonder if it's Toni. Oh my God, Toni. The look on her face when I told her I didn't want a relationship with her. Astonishment, sadness, mortification. It went through so many phases in that split second and I... I had to leave. Run. I couldn't bear to see her.

I couldn't bear to hear her try to convince me that we would work. That she understands. That she loves me.

It didn't matter that I believed her. That I knew she wasn't trying to control me. The echoes of my relationship with Shae were too strong and I did what I knew I had to do. Protect myself. Put myself first. And crush Toni in the process.

I feel Willa re-enter the room, and hear the door close.

"Here," she says.

I look up and she's holding a glass of water.

"Thank you."

The cold liquid sluices down my throat and almost quenches the fire of shame and guilt roaring in my veins. But it's too strong. The ember is still there, waiting for a burst of emotion to light it again.

"I told Greta that Mom had suddenly shown up in Denver and wondered where we were."

I look at her in confusion.

"I know, stupid lie. Toni had apparently just left the house like a bat out of hell, and, well, she saw what happened before."

"What did she say?"

"She said it was probably a good idea, to drive safe, and she will see us on January 2."

"To terminate our contract, probably."

"Oh no. Before I made it to the stairs she clarified that. Business as usual." Willa clears her throat. "Let's get out of here."

We are ready to go in ten minutes.

When we leave there is no one around to say goodbye to.

CHAPTER TWENTY-SIX

AUDREY

I'm not sure what to expect when we return to the office on January 2, but I didn't expect everything to be so normal. My world had shifted, seismically, but all anyone could talk about was their holidays, their families, their presents, vacations, food, desserts, and work.

That is, Greta was all about work.

"How do you think she'll be today?" I asked Willa when we were on the way to Greta's office for our morning meeting.

"All business. She won't mention a word unless you do, and I suggest you don't," Willa said, and pushed through Greta's office door.

On the other side of the door the quiet, introspective Willa of the last week was gone. My sister was back, full of life and making jokes, bringing her irrepressible energy into every room she walks into.

The car ride back to Denver from Aspen had been silent. I didn't want to talk and Willa didn't push. Maybe she didn't want to talk, either. She was driving and our rule since we got our driver's licenses when we were sixteen was the driver controls the radio. It had been set to the satellite radio holiday station for weeks. When Perry Como started singing about dreaming of a white Christmas, she turned the radio off completely, and we drove the remaining hours in complete silence.

I'm not an idiot. I know something happened between Willa and Greta that weekend, but they are doing a stellar job pretending otherwise.

At the office, a few weeks into the new year, Willa and Greta are back to their old selves: Willa pushing Greta's boundaries and Greta valiantly holding the professional lines she's drawn. Greta has an amazing poker face. Willa not so much, but that might be a twin thing. I've caught Greta gazing at her with a puzzled expression more than once. Willa, for her part, has returned to rolling her eyes behind Greta's back. I don't think she will ever renew the offer to distract Greta for me and Toni. Not that she's needed to, because Toni hasn't been back into the office since Christmas.

News swept the office that Toni moved up her trip to South America, and is going to be in the office occasionally and unpredictably. That was not nearly enough information for me. When Greta and I were finished with a meeting, I took a deep breath and asked about Toni for the first time in a month.

"Toni's in South America?" I asked while putting my meeting notes and computer in my bag, hoping for nonchalance, but my voice went up an octave at the end of my innocent question, ruining my plans.

"Yes." Greta didn't take her attention from her computer. Most likely she was typing notes about our meeting that would land in my inbox in five minutes. I consider myself organized, diligent, and responsible, but Greta takes it all to the next level.

"Do you know when she will be back?"

Greta's hands stilled, but remained on her keyboard. She

looked at me. "Audrey, I appreciate the help you gave Toni early on, but she's not part of your project, and I think it would be best for everyone concerned if you focus on the job you are contracted to do."

I've been dressed down by employers before, with varying responses on my part from indignation to embarrassment and everything in between. I was properly chastised, and deservedly so, but what I saw when I looked closely at Greta Giordani was not the CEO of a company recently tapped by *Fortune* magazine as the Best Family-Run Business in the US, but a protective sister using all the self-control she possessed to not rip off the face of the woman who broke her little sister's heart.

"You're absolutely correct," I said quickly, to hide the smile that wanted to spread across my face. Toni would be so jazzed to see Greta bowing up on me to protect her. In that moment, I saw Toni's expression the night she inadvertently pitched to Greta and saw Greta's genuine interest. *I can't wait to tell Toni*, I thought, before reality came crashing down again.

After my initial explanation, Willa hasn't asked me about what happened again. At first I was thankful, but now I'm hurt. I need my sister, and she's avoiding me, acting like she doesn't care.

Weeks pass with still no sign of Toni at the office. Valentine's Day, a holiday I've always secretly loved but have never been with a partner who feels the same, comes and goes. Of course, I don't expect to hear from Toni; we aren't a couple. But my mind, traitor that it is, imagines what kind of girlfriend Toni would be on Valentine's Day. Breakfast in bed, after a very long night of making love and earth-shattering orgasms (because of course she would want to start celebrating at midnight), a homemade card because there wasn't one that was just right at the drugstore, chocolates and flowers. My present to her would have been a coupon good for one outdoor hike, rated easy to moderate, preferably on a level trail, and less than five miles, spending the day in bed making love and talking. Maybe a weekend trip to Napa. I've always wanted to go and never have. Huh. I don't even know if Toni likes wine.

Our project with Fourteener Sports is half over, and on track to finish on time. Greta, happy with how everything is progressing, calls in a favor and gets Willa and me on the list for the opening night of the next big thing in the Denver restaurant scene, a gin distillery and farm-to-table restaurant called Gin and Bear it. Willa and I are sipping our gin and tonics and munching on the canapés being passed around when I see Toni's best friend, Max, walk in the door. My heart leaps to my throat, hoping that Toni is going to walk in behind her. Instead, it's someone I don't know.

Willa follows my gaze and sees Max notice me and stare daggers in my direction. I refuse to turn away or avert my eyes.

"Someone doesn't like you," Willa says.

"No kidding." When Max finally wanders out of my line of sight I let out a small sigh of relief. "Did I tell you that it was her apartment Toni took me to that first night?"

"No."

"We slept in Max's bed, apparently."

"Huh," Willa says, checking her phone for the fifth time in five minutes.

"That's all you have to say? Huh?"

Willa levels her gaze at me. "What do you want me to say, Audrey?"

"I don't know, show a little interest, at least."

"In your one-night stand? Or two-night stand, I guess. Why? You broke it off with her before it started. There's not a lot to talk about. You aren't ready for a relationship, and you broke Toni's heart. It's pretty simple."

"It sounds so cruel when you say it like that."

"Well, it was a little cruel," Willa snaps.

"I was upfront with her about what I wanted," I say. "And she agreed to it."

"If you didn't do anything wrong, then stop moping around like you got your heart broken, Audrey. No one cares or feels sorry for you. Instead, you should feel bad about leading Toni on and then crushing her heart like a bug under your shoe. All Toni wanted, from what I can tell, was a chance with you, and you shut it down before anything could even really start."

"That is completely unfair," I say.

Willa looks at her phone again. "Finally." She puts her phone in her bag, downs her gin and tonic and puts the glass on the bar table with a snap. "I've gotta go."

"What? You can't say that shit to me and then just leave," I say.

She stands. "Actually, yes I can."

"Where are you going?"

"Not that it's any of your business, but I have a date."

Willa hasn't dated in years, and we've been working non-stop since December. "A date? Since when? How did you meet? Who is he?"

"On an app, and her name is Amanda."

My mouth drops open in shock. Willa is going on a date with a woman?

Willa scoffs. "Yeah, I've been going through it, too, but you've had your head too far up your ass to care. See you at home. Don't wait up."

I watch Willa weave her way through the crowd until she's lost from sight, too flabbergasted to move.

I feel as if I've been punched in the gut. Leave it to my twin, my best friend, to give it to me straight, and in the most brutal way possible, about how I'm being self-indulgent on two fronts. I'm not sure "moping around" is the best descriptor of what I've been doing, but Willa is right, I handled everything with Toni wrong in Aspen. It's hard to regret sleeping with her, but we should have slowed down. Waited. But we didn't, and I'm mostly to blame for that. I'm entirely to blame for my knee-jerk reaction to her kissing me, and her declarations after. How I could be so passive for so long with Shae, who treated me like dirt, and so immediate and cruel with Toni, who treated me like a queen and only wanted to love me, is going to take some deep introspection to work out. Apologizing to Toni as soon as possible is the first step.

And Willa needs me—has needed me for weeks—and I haven't been there for her. I feel lower than chewing gum on the bottom of a sneaker. If Willa is questioning or exploring her sexuality because of something that happened in Aspen... she has to be feeling very confused. I thought her disinterest was a sign that she was sick of me talking about Toni. Instead, she's going through something herself, and has been putting her emotional needs before mine for the first time... ever? God, I'm such a heel.

I've got to try to catch her, to apologize. I gather my purse and loop it across my body.

"Are you leaving?" I look up and see Greta standing in front of me with a drink in her hand. "Where's Willa?"

"She, um, left. She had somewhere to be."

"Oh." Greta is clearly disappointed. "Sorry I was late. Are you leaving?"

"Um." I look toward the door. I want to go and get started on my penance now, but Greta went to the trouble to get us into this party, and I should at least share a drink with her. "Not since you're here." I sit back down at the table and Greta takes Willa's seat. "This place is great," I say.

"It is," Greta says. "The owner is a friend of mine."

"Oh," I say. "How do you know each other?"

"College."

"Oh."

We both take sips of our drinks and look around. I don't

know about Greta, but I'm searching desperately for something to say. For the first time since I've known her, things are awkward. We've never been in a social situation just the two of us, and Willa and Toni's absence hangs heavily between us. I just want to be alone to think, to figure out what to do, how to make things right with Willa.

"When was the last time you saw Shae?" Greta asks.

"At the Christmas party. Why?"

"Here she comes."

I turn and there Shae is, making a beeline for our table, all her little minions following in a row. She says something to Lisa, the woman just behind her, and the hangers-on break off and go to the bar.

"Hey, Audrey. Greta, good to see you, too." She looks between us, a knowing leer on her face.

I don't know what to say. It's not good to see her, so I stay silent. Greta does as well.

"I heard about the upcoming *Fortune* magazine feature, Greta. Congratulations."

"Thank you," she says.

"That'll be a nice addition for your CV, Audrey. But those lists are decided a year out, so everyone will know that your consulting didn't have anything to do with it. I'm sure dating Greta will help you get business in the future, though."

"We aren't dating," Greta and I say at the same time, though out of sync so it sounds garbled.

"This certainly looks like a date," Shae says. "And Toni's certainly moved on."

"What do you mean?" I say, my stomach twisting into a knot of dread.

"I saw her at Dewey's and you definitely weren't the woman with her tongue down Toni's throat."

My own throat closes up. I can't swallow, and I can barely breathe. But the last thing I want is for Shae to see that. I look at

Greta for confirmation or denial of what Shae said, but she's looking down at her drink, avoiding my eyes.

Of course Toni's moved on. Why shouldn't she? I'm sure my reaction and the things I said made her rethink her feelings for me and rightly so. My brain says this is what I wanted, but my heart has other ideas.

"Oh, shit," Shae says, covering her mouth and laughing.

Shae always could read me like a book. A children's book. The board ones that are indestructible and have one word and a big photo on each page so newborns can see it clearly. Shae is loving this and I want to die.

"Don't tell me your new girlfriend was cheating on you at Dewey's like your old one. Wow, you really do have a type, don't you?" Shae says.

"No, I don't," I miraculously manage to say in a mostly steady voice. Thank God the music has been turned up in the last thirty minutes. "Toni and I are not seeing each other and we've never been girlfriends. What she does and with whom is none of my business, nor do I care." The lie tastes like chalk in my mouth.

Shae laughs. "Keep telling yourself that. Maybe eventually you'll believe it. Nice chat," she says, and winks at me.

When Shae turns her back, I immediately open my phone and go to Instagram. If Toni really is over me, the proof will be there.

"Audrey, don't." Greta reaches her hand out to cover my phone.

I pull it away. My finger swipes up through Toni's feed, my stomach falling further with each new post I see of her, sliding right back into her nomadic lifestyle. The number of posts of her jumping off cliffs, hiking, and reviewing gear are dwarfed by the posts of her with different beautiful women apparently having the time of her life.

CHAPTER TWENTY-SEVEN

TONI

I collapse on my new bed and exhale.

"God, moving is tiring," I say.

"You haven't even moved. I have," Max says. She pirouettes and plops down beside me.

We stare up at the ceiling of what used to be Max's bedroom but is now mine, and study the crack in the ceiling.

"Should I worry about that?" I ask.

"Landlord says nope, so you probably should," Max says.

"Good thing I'm on the top floor."

"Yeah, you won't say that when you're hauling groceries up three flights of stairs."

After Christmas, Max had made good on her promise to find a new place and sub-lease this apartment to me. She left most of the furniture, which had been handed down to her from the previous tenant, and decorated her new place to fit her style, which is mostly black Ikea furniture with clean lines and matching Billy bookshelves along the walls that she's eager to fill with books. We both wanted new couches and went shopping together, splurging on super plush ones that you could waste away an evening marathoning a nature documentary (me) or reading horror novels and paranormal romance (Max).

It's the perfect set-up. I love the neighborhood and the rent is affordable enough (though not cheap) that I don't feel like I am wasting money while traveling around the world for my job.

Max looks at me. "How are you doing?"

"I'm good. Great."

"How are you really doing?"

I sigh and groan. "I'm tired and I have to put the fucking sheets on before I can go to bed."

"Come on. I'll help." Max gets up and holds out her hands to me. I take them and she drags me up off my new mattress. She gets the sheets out of the trunk against the wall and throws a fitted sheet at me. I look at it. Powder blue.

"Are these the—"

"Yes."

I go to the trunk and get another set of sheets.

"Well, that's a better answer to my question," Max says drily.

I don't say anything, because what is there to say? It's been over two months since Audrey Adams broke my heart, and it still feels like there is an open, festering wound in my chest. But I'm not going to tell Max that. Or anyone. I'm sure everyone is as tired of hearing me talk about my heartbreak as I am of talking about it.

Valentine's Day was particularly brutal, which is why I made sure to be as far away from Denver and the Fourteener Sports office as possible. New Zealand is beautiful in February, by the way.

We are putting on the pillowcases when I ask, "How was the opening last night?"

"Good. Glad you didn't go, though."

"Why?"

"Audrey and Willa were there."

"Oh." I feel sick to my stomach with longing at the mere sound of her name. I am so pathetic.

I toss both pillows against the headboard and Max throws the down duvet over the top of the bed.

"How did she look?" I say. "Audrey."

Max puts her hands on her hips and cocks one out to the side, her signature stance, and blows her heavy bangs out of her eyes. She needs a trim.

"Come on," I say.

She knows what I'm talking about without asking and follows me into the bathroom. She sits on the side of the tub while I get everything ready: a towel on her lap, a bath mat below her feet, a spray bottle, two pairs of scissors, and a comb.

I spray her bangs with water, comb them down, then start to trim. I've been cutting Max's bangs for as long as we can remember. The first time they were a little crooked, but not by much. It took her parents a week to realize her bangs had been cut, and not by Max's mom. I'd watched Linda do it enough that I figured how hard could it be. Turns out, it wasn't that hard, and I've been doing it ever since. We were five.

"Well?" I say, concentrating on getting a straight line.

"No way I'm talking about her when you have a sharp object in your hand."

"I'm fine," I say. I comb her bangs, pull them through my fingers, and snip off the ends. "Besides, you would look totally badass in an eyepatch. Your business would go through the roof. Butch Bartender's New Eyepatch Brings All the Babes to the Bar. News at Six."

"Excuse me, I'm not butch, I'm soft butch, and I would totally rock an eyepatch. But I've recently been told I have eyes *that will haunt women's souls* so I'd kinda like to keep them."

I chuckle. "That's pretty over the top."

"It's borderline cheesy but who the fuck cares when it's

being delivered by a woman with that voice and that body and all the skills."

I stop cutting. "Was this last night?" I ask.

"Until mid-morning, yes."

"Christ on a cracker, Max. Why are you here helping me make my bed on your day off?"

"Because I said I'd be here." Her expression softens. "I want to be here."

I smile. "You don't have to babysit me. I'm not going to do anything drastic."

Max's head jerks back. "Swear to God, that thought never crossed my mind."

"Good. We're done." I put up the scissors while Max tries to clean up the hair without getting it all over the floor. "Don't worry. I got a hand-held vacuum."

"Oh, OK." Max flicks the towel and little bits of black hair float down to the floor like the saddest confetti party you've ever seen.

"Well, I didn't mean to do that."

"Payback for getting laid in my bed."

"I washed the sheets," I say. I click off the bathroom light and we amble into the living room. Max plops down on my couch, which is exactly like her couch. I go into the kitchen to get us a drink. "Come on. How was Audrey?"

"I didn't talk to her, but she looked good. Maybe a little pale." I hand Max a beer. She takes a drink. "But that's probably because I gave her the best friend death stare."

"Max."

"I'll give her credit, she never moved. Just sat right there in my line of sight and took it."

"Took it as in she was uncomfortable and thought she deserved it? Or took it as in you're not going to beat me, bitch, bring it on?"

Max's beer stops right before it gets to her lips. She drops it down and rests it on her thigh. "I have no idea which answer you want."

"Um, the truth?"

Max finally takes the drink, swallows, then says, "You know, a little bit of both, but more of the second. That's when Shae showed up."

"What? What happened?"

"Not a thing. They talked, Shae went to hang out with her minions, Audrey left the bar, and I met a gorgeous redhead." The last little bit elicits a huge grin.

This is the only firsthand information I've gotten from anyone about Audrey since Christmas and I am desperate for more. What was she wearing? Was her hair still short or had it gotten longer? What did she smell like?

OK, that last one is admittedly weird. I can't ask any of the questions, unless I want to be outed as a liar about how great I am.

My doorbell rings, startling us both.

"Expecting someone?" Max says.

"Only you."

The moment before I open the door a small hope that it's Audrey flits through my heart. I try not to show my disappointment when Greta stands in the hall, a smile on her face, and an enormous plant in her arms.

"Happy housewarming."

My sister is here. Bringing me a plant. Smiling at me. Honestly, it's better than if it was Audrey.

Well, almost better. It's pretty fucking great considering five months ago we barely tolerated each other.

"Greta, hey. Here, let me take that."

"Thanks. I thought I was in pretty good shape but carrying that up three flights of stairs made me realize I need to up the resistance on my climbing machine."

"Or, you could come hiking with me one weekend."

"Oh, hey, Max," Greta says.

"Hey, Greta," Max says, and manages not to drool all over my new couch. "Wanna beer?"

"Sure, but I can get it." Greta puts her purse down and goes into the kitchen. "Today your day off?"

I stand in the middle of the room, holding the plant and looking around wondering where to put it. Greta sees me and points. "Over by the window, Toni."

I follow her instructions because, as much as I love trees in nature, I've never been able to keep a plant alive. I decide to not tell Greta that, put the plant down, and turn it so that the bushy part faces the room.

The three of us chat for a bit, Greta sitting in the corner of my new couch with her shoes off and her legs pulled up underneath her, angled toward Max and talking about business and the opening last night. I sit on the matching chair (I know, so bougie), watch them, and wish Audrey and Willa were here, too.

I've not only been grieving the loss of Audrey, but the loss of the four of us, the friendship we'd built over the weeks we worked together. It was amazing how easily we all got along, how our personalities meshed and complemented each other. There was never a lull in our conversations, and no one dominated. It had pulled Greta out of the shell she'd created over the years to protect her from the stress and anxiety of being in charge. At least, that's how I think of Business Greta, especially when I see her like this, relaxed and comfortable and engaged.

"I better go," Max says. She stands and stretches her arms over her head, her shirt riding up and showing the pale skin of her stomach, with an enormous hickey next to the navel. My eyes go wide, and I look at Greta to see if she noticed. She's looking at the plant by the window, completely uninterested in Max's little display. Max looks a little disappointed, which means she did that for Greta's benefit. Poor Max. She's never gonna give up, I guess.

I walk my friend to the door and as soon as the door closes behind her, Greta says, "Toni, it's time."

"For another beer?" I ask.

"For you to come back into the office."

"No. I'm not ready."

"You're mistaking this for a suggestion. This is your boss telling you that you need to be at the office at nine a.m. tomorrow morning for the staff meeting. And be ready to give everyone an update on what you've been doing for the last two months."

"Greta, I—"

Greta holds her finger up. "I'm not done."

"Should I sit back down?"

"Probably."

I sit on the couch and angle myself toward my sister.

"*I* want you back in the office," she says.

I expected Greta to give me a spiel about my responsibilities, setting an example for the other employees, and showing Audrey that she hadn't crushed me. I absolutely did not expect her to lead with this. I'm too stunned to speak, but Greta doesn't give me much time to, anyway, before barreling on.

"I miss having you around. You bring a needed energy to Fourteener Sports. Willa makes up for it a bit, but she's a contractor and will be leaving in a few months. And, she's not family." Greta swallows, takes a drink of her beer, and realizes it's empty. "Maybe I will take another one." Her voice is a little raspy.

I rise without a word, get us two fresh beers, and return.

Greta takes a long drink and pauses, I think, to gather her thoughts. Instead, she hits her chest lightly with her fist and lets out one of the loudest burps I've ever heard. Her eyes are wide when she looks at me. "Sorry."

I can't help it, I fall over laughing onto my stupidly expensive, decadently comfortable couch.

"If you tell a soul about that I will deny it," she says.

I'm not looking at her but I hear the laughter in her voice. I sit back up, and see Greta grinning, with a slight blush on her face.

"Oh, you know I'm going to break that story out when you least expect it."

She rolls her eyes, but she's still grinning. "I'm sure you will pick the worst possible moment."

"Absolutely. What are little sisters for?"

Greta shakes her head, takes another drink. "I've hired a Marketing and PR firm to take advantage of this whole *Fortune* magazine thing, and I want you involved in the development of our strategy, since you're one half of the new face of Fourteener Sports."

"Who's the other? Ned?"

"Yes. Absolutely." She reaches out and touches my leg. "You're doing a great job with the adventure division, working from home and on the road. Which is a little surprising, considering your Instagram." She raises an eyebrow.

"I've been wondering when you'd mention that."

Greta shrugs. "You've been doing your job so there wasn't a point, but I am curious. Are you getting any sleep at all?"

"Yeah, about that. They're all strangers."

Greta doesn't react for a beat. "Aren't they always?"

"OK, fair. But, um, I don't sleep with them. Not lately. The women. The strangers. I ask them to take a photo with me, buy them a drink, chat a little, maybe, then send them on their way."

Greta furrows her brow then laughs. "What? Why?"

"I'm not interested."

"Did Audrey's rejection turn you straight?"

"God, no. *Gross.* I'll go out, have a beer or two then go back wherever I'm staying."

"You're trying to make Audrey jealous."

I blush to my roots. "I wasn't at first. I was really trying to move on. But I just..." *None of them were Audrey*, I think. They didn't feel like her or sound like her when I touched them. They didn't look at me like Audrey did, either. Remembering the way Audrey looked at me is what was, and is, most confusing. Not only when we were making love, but when I would catch her at random times during the day. There was always such... the stupid romantic part of me thought love, but now I don't know what to call it. Those expressions are what torture me the most.

"Toni?" Greta says softly.

I shake the image of Audrey out of my mind. "It was too soon. I know posting those photos was childish and immature, but yeah. I wanted her to see that I'm not holed up somewhere licking my wounds, even if it's not the whole truth."

"That's pretty passive-aggressive, which I don't approve of as a rule. For this, I'll make an exception." She studies me for a moment, chewing on her bottom lip.

"What?"

She shakes her head once. "Nothing. Back to business. Don't take what I'm about to say as me wanting to take over your department."

I bristle. I knew this would come eventually.

"I do want to be more in the loop, but more than that, I want our employees to see you are the one making this happen. That you're taking your idea and running with it. Making it a success. It's important that they see, and believe, that we are equal partners."

"Wha... did you just say equal partners?"

"Yes, of course. We've always had equal shares, but I want this to be a true professional partnership. You know how important the income from your division is going to be to us."

"Right. Professionally." I'm surprised by the stab of disappointment I feel, and do my best to hide it by taking a drink.

"Hey," Greta says.

I look up at her and know she sees right through me.

"You're doing a fantastic job, but that's not the main reason I want you in the office. I want my *sister* beside me. It's been hell trying to be the fun one at work," she says, humor sparking in her eyes. "I rather liked being an ice queen. I need you to come back and take some of the pressure off me." Her cheeks puff out when she blows out a dramatic breath. "It's exhausting. I don't know how you and Willa do it."

I suppress a smile. I know without a doubt that no one in that office will say that Greta has been the fun one the last two months.

"OK," I say. "I'll be there tomorrow. Ready to go at nine a.m."

"You will?"

"Absolutely. I need to save everyone from your sad attempts at being the fun one."

She lifts her head up to the sky. "Thank you, baby Jesus."

"But you might have forgotten I leave for New Zealand again on Tuesday."

Greta squinches up her nose. "I did forget." She waves her hand away. "Come to the meeting anyway. Everyone misses you."

She takes her empty beer bottle to the kitchen and is getting ready to leave. I can't let her leave without knowing.

"Has, um, Audrey asked about me?"

Greta adjusts the strap of her purse on her shoulder before meeting my gaze. "Yes. Once."

"Oh." Only once? Jesus, I was hoping for a bit more than that.

"She got the message that she needed to focus on doing her fucking job and not asking about you."

My head jerks back at the heat in Greta's voice. "Did you say that to her?"

"Not in those words, no. But my tone of voice got the point across. Trust me." She turns at the door. "Don't worry about having a big presentation tomorrow. I know this is short notice."

"Nope, it's no problem. I'll have something ready."

Greta nods and is out the door when she stops and turns around. "Is it all pretending to the world? That you're over her?"

"Mostly. I cycle through the stages of grief pretty regularly." I can't tell Greta about the random crying jags I go on because they're just mortifying. You'd think I was getting out of a ten-year relationship instead of one that hadn't officially started and consisted of two hook-ups and weeks of flirting.

Greta raises her eyebrows. "The stages of grief?"

"Yes. I've had my heart broken, Greta. For the first time."

Greta's expression softens. "What stage are you in right now?"

"This moment? Sadness."

"But that can change?"

My sister has obviously never had her heart broken. It's a new experience for me, too.

"Yes, but it's happening less and less. I'm more in the resignation phase than anything."

"Maybe you shouldn't come back to the office," Greta says.

"No, I'll come," I say, surprising myself. But it feels right to say it. I need to move forward, and my sister wants me in the office, with her as an equal partner. "I can't avoid Audrey forever."

CHAPTER TWENTY-EIGHT

AUDREY

When I got home from the restaurant, I spent hours scrolling back and forth through Toni's social media since Christmas, especially Instagram where she was most active. When we returned home from Aspen, I'd promised myself I wouldn't stalk her online. What was done was done and it was time for both of us to move on. It didn't take long for work to take over my life and for my curiosity about Toni and what she was doing to only encroach on my thoughts once an hour or so instead of every time I saw something at the office that reminded me of her. (*Everything* at the office reminded me of her. A ballpoint pen reminded me of her.) Obviously, I avoided the conference room at all costs.

Toni's presence was felt despite not being in the office. Longtime employees, and most Fourteener Sports employees were longtime employees, all had Toni stories. Universally funny, oftentimes nerve-racking. My palms would sweat with fear when Ned talked about some of the more extreme stunts Toni pulled as a child, despite knowing that Toni would live through each and every harebrained one of them. There were an almost equal amount of Greta stories. It was an open secret that Toni was motivated to go one step further than Greta to prove herself. I'd never realized that meant that Greta had her own thick volume of athletic achievements, and an equal amount of admiration and respect from her employees. Every day I understood why Willa felt at home here, why she might want to stay.

And how I might have taken that opportunity away from her.

I'm in the kitchen making French toast on Sunday morning, soaking thick slices of French bread in a cinnamon-flavored egg mixture, when Willa walks out of her bedroom.

Her eyes light up. "French toast?"

"Yep." I pour her a cup of coffee and set it on the kitchen island. She sits on a stool, takes a fortifying sip, and gazes at me over the rim. She surveys the cut fruit, French toast, coffee, and a cute little bouquet of flowers I saw when checking out at Whole Foods late last night. She raises one eyebrow and I'm busted.

"OK, I went overboard."

"Ya think?"

"Honestly? Probably not. I have a lot to apologize for."

Willa hums a response, drinks her coffee, and remains silent.

"I shouldn't have slept with Toni so soon. I handled her kissing me and telling me she loved me horribly, and I've been so self-absorbed since I've ignored that you're going through your own stuff and need me to be here for you."

I exhale, and Willa remains silent. She puts her mug down carefully and says, "Acknowledging all the ways you fucked everything up isn't the same as apologizing for all the ways you fucked everything up."

"You're right. I'm sorry, Willa. You have every right to be

angry with me. You've been my rock for so long, supporting me through everything with Shae, always putting me first, that I came to expect it. Not intentionally, because I absolutely don't think I'm your responsibility. I don't want to be, and I don't want you to feel like I am. But, yeah. You've been selfless and I've been self-absorbed and I'm really, really sorry. I love you more than anyone on this earth, and it kills me to know that you've been hurting and didn't want to come to me about it, that I wasn't your person. It's my fault I wasn't. But I'm here now, and forever. Whatever you need, whenever you need it."

"We'll start with a hug, then French toast."

I go around the counter and, for the first time in a long time, pull my sister into an embrace. She collapses into me and buries her head in my shoulder. She shakes slightly, and I hold her tighter.

"I'm so sorry, Willa."

She pulls back and sniffs loudly. Her eyes are red and watery. "Stop apologizing. I forgive you."

"Do you want to talk about what happened with you and Greta?"

"No, actually."

"Oh. OK." The denial stings, but this isn't about me.

"I'm over it," she says. My expression must show my skepticism because she amends, "Mostly. I just don't want to go back there."

Jesus, what the hell happened? I think.

"We didn't sleep together," Willa says. "We had a moment, it passed, and now we've moved on."

I'm pretty sure that's the biggest oversimplification in the history of the world, but I don't press.

"Don't worry, I'll tell you eventually," Willa says. I exhale loudly in relief and Willa laughs. "I'm not gonna lie, I'm holding back to torture you a bit."

"Mission accomplished."

"You deserve it."

"I totally do."

"I'm sorry for what I said to you last night," Willa says. "I mean, you needed to hear it, obviously, but I could have been a little gentler about it."

"I probably wouldn't have gotten the message if you were."

"True."

We eat for a few minutes and I'm ginning up the courage to ask her about her date when Willa says, "I channeled my anger with Greta toward how you treated Toni because there are some... slight similarities."

Willa isn't looking at me so I know not to probe too directly. "Oh?"

"Very slight. More of a turn your head and squint kind of similarities."

I hum my response, hoping that Willa will elaborate. When she remains silent I ask the question I've been dying to ask for hours.

"So, how was your date?"

Willa glances up at me. "Let's just say I have a new friend, and only a friend. Probably more of a business contact."

"Were you not attracted to her?"

"Oh, no. She's a smokeshow," Willa says. "But she was also terrifying."

"In what way?"

"A very sexy way."

I press my lips together to keep from smiling.

"I'm definitely not ready for that," Willa says. "Once I told her, she dropped the whole *I want to eat you for breakfast* facade and we had a great time."

"Well, it was good for you to get out there again."

"Agreed. Now, enough about that. How long did you stay last night? Did Greta ever show?"

I fill her in on seeing Shae and the news about Toni.

"Yeah," she says slowly. "I've been keeping up with her social media, too. I wasn't trying to punish you by not telling you. I knew you couldn't take the idea of Toni being over everything so soon, so I kept my mouth shut."

"That's not it," I say. "I'm glad she's moved on. She needs to move on. I just hate how I did it. That I was cruel."

"You're a better woman than I am, because I would be livid," Willa says.

"I don't have any right to be, though, do I? I broke it off, whatever there was to break off."

"Oh please," Willa says. "Don't pretend you weren't half in love with her, Audrey. Not with me. You can say whatever shit you want to the world, but not to me."

I pick at my fruit as my heart clenches in my chest. "You're right," I say softly. "When I was saying those cruel things, watching Toni's face collapse, the other side of my brain was screaming *What the fuck are you doing, this is wrong, this woman is worth it.*" I lift my eyes to meet Willa's. "It was too much too soon. I wasn't ready."

Willa's eyes narrow and her mouth goes tight. I've hit a nerve. I'm not sure what she's going to say when she opens her mouth.

"And now? If you were to see Toni tomorrow, what would you do?"

My heart leaps at the thought of seeing Toni, looking into those blue eyes, seeing her sitting on the corner of someone's desk, telling a story and laughing, looking at me like I'm her Christmas puppy. The way just being around her relaxes me and makes me happy.

"I have absolutely no clue."

I'm running late, which I never do. But for some reason only God knows I decided to go to yoga this morning for the first time in months. My plan to get ready there was ruined when I opened my bag to shower and saw no makeup and no fresh bra. By the time I ran home to get ready, I had to fight traffic to get to the office and I make it to my desk at 08:55, a good hour later than normal. I texted Willa, so everyone knows I'm on my way. Being late is my biggest pet peeve and I'm almost running down the hall to make the Monday staff meeting, looking down at my phone to check the time, three minutes to go, and do not see the person coming out of the break room.

We collide at full force, knocking my phone across the hall, my bag off my shoulder, and spilling coffee all over the other person's shirt.

"Shit," we say at the same time, before everything freezes.

I know who I'm going to see before our eyes meet and, based on her expression, she did, too.

My entire body lights up with joy at the sight of her, those sparkling blue eyes, the flyaway hair that can never be tamed by her braid, the curve of her full bottom lip. And then she smiles at me, open and unreserved and full of happiness, like she used to every time she saw me, and I am bowled over with an absolute certainty.

I am in love with Toni Danzig.

The relief is so palpable I laugh and grin.

Toni mistakes it for something else and joins in. "Yeah, we gotta stop meeting like this."

It's then that I notice that it's her shirt covered in coffee this time. "Oh my God I'm so sorry."

"It's fine. It's flannel. Practically indestructible." She turns back into the break room to refill her cup.

I follow her, the fifteen people waiting in the conference room forgotten. "It's good to see you," I say. "I didn't know you were going to be in the office."

With a new cup, she turns. "I didn't either until last night. Greta made a pretty convincing case, and it was time." She looks me up and down, but there's no heat, no wanting in her expression. It's very different from her smile moments before. "How are you?"

"Besides running late, I'm good. Pretty good. Busy with work."

"Yeah."

We stand there, at a loss as to what to say next.

"I'm sorry," I blurt.

"Really, it's OK, Audrey." Toni lifts her shirt and takes a sniff. "Though I don't really want to smell like coffee all day." She puts the cup down and, without unbuttoning the shirt, whips it off over her head. For a split second I think I'm going to see those wonderful abs again and, in a way, I do. Toni is wearing a form-fitting base layer in Fourteener blue that hugs every single one of her curves. It's like the shirt was vacuum sealed onto her body and I feel so lightheaded I think I'm going to faint.

"Do you want some coffee? Or cider?" Toni offers.

Apparently she's oblivious to the effect she's having on me, but how the fuck is that possible? My mouth is gaping open. I know this because when I shut it my back teeth click together.

"Yes, coffee would be great."

She drapes her soiled flannel across the back of a chair and returns to the coffee bar, her back to me, giving me a clear view of her ass in those confounded hiking pants. Before she reaches for the coffee, she pulls the long sleeves of her shirt halfway up her forearms.

Someone is playing very dirty.

"Here you go," she says. She sets the cup down on the table. "See you in there."

"Wait," I say, touching her arm. Energy hums from her arm through my hand like a current. She stops and looks at me with her eyes, electric blue against the color of her shirt. She shifts her arm so that we aren't touching, and my stomach falls. "I wasn't apologizing for the shirt, though I am sorry for that." OK, that's a total lie because oh my God I will never regret Toni taking off that boxy flannel shirt. "I was apologizing for Christmas Eve."

Her expression goes blank. "Oh. If it's all the same, I'd rather just leave the past in the past."

"Oh, but I—"

"You were right. It was too much too soon, and that's on me. You were right about a lot of it, I see that now. You weren't ready for anything serious, and I mean, who can blame you after that shitshow with Shae? And I didn't think I could handle just having fun. With you. We're just at two different points in our life. We would have had to work really hard to make us work and who wants to do that?" She shakes her head. "I don't. Over the last couple of months, I realized I really liked my life, my social life, the way it was. So, really. It's all good." She holds out her hand. "Friends?"

"Um, yeah." I reach out to shake Toni's hand in a daze, and not in the trippy LSD peace love and happiness kind of daze. Shake her hand, for God's sake! When what I wanted to do five minutes ago was to push her up against the wall and shove my tongue down her throat.

Her hand is strong and thin, with a ridge of calluses where the palm meets her fingers, but her touch is gentle, as if she's afraid of the contact. As well she should be. Her eyes darken with an expression I know very well, and a lightning bolt of desire strikes deep inside me. She holds my gaze for a second, two, then drops it to my lips.

"Who knows," she says, barely above a whisper. Her gaze travels back to meet mine. "Maybe we will see each other across the room in a crowded bar again soon." She drops my hand, steps back, and grins. "Could be fun."

"Hey, where's my coffee?" Willa appears in the door. "Oh,

hey, Auds, didn't realize you made it. Come on. We're waiting on you two."

Toni hands my sister the forgotten mug. "Here you go, Miranda Priestly."

"I'll take that as a compliment," Willa says. I can still hear her voice as they walk down the hall. "Though I always saw myself more as the Emily Blunt character."

Toni laughs. "No way in hell."

What in the world just happened here?

It takes every ounce of energy and effort I have to put one foot in front of the other and follow them. I have fifteen seconds to pull myself together before I walk into the conference room.

I'm not sure I'll be able to do it in a lifetime.

CHAPTER TWENTY-NINE

AUDREY

I walk into the Chicken Head Saloon and let my eyes adjust to the dark. With a name like the Chicken Head I have no idea what kind of decorative kitsch is going to greet me, though I figure there will be at least one "Eggs for Sale" sign somewhere on the walls. Instead, the walls are covered with antique climbing gear and black-and-white photos of people in Victorian clothes posing on glaciers and next to makeshift flags stuck into rocky outcroppings on top of a mountain.

I'm sure there's a connection between the chicken head on the sign and all of this, but I have no idea what it is and, frankly, I don't care. I scan the bar, which looks like a British pub and smells like stale beer and patchouli, looking for Toni. It's almost deserted, not surprising for a Monday night at the end of February. There are a couple of men sitting with a barstool open between them, not talking but obviously together, an abandoned beer at the end of the bar in the back, and two couples playing darts on the other side of the bar. No one else.

I exhale. It was a shot in the dark anyway. But after the comment Toni made in the break room, it was a shot I had to take, especially when I learned Toni is leaving the country tomorrow for at least two weeks.

Might as well have a drink while I'm here. I pick a stool at the short end of the U-shaped bar and order a gin and tonic.

"Do you have cucumber? For the drink?" I ask.

He's old and grizzled with a beard that looks like it hasn't been trimmed since this building was built in the nineteenth century. He looks at me through narrowed blue eyes and doesn't answer.

"Lime is fine. Thanks."

I look around while I wait for my drink. So, this is Toni's regular bar. Huh. I suppose she feels at home here surrounded by all the climbing stuff and it does have a certain charm if you don't mind the sticky bar, uneven barstools, and overly chatty bartender.

He lays a napkin down on the bar and puts my drink on it.

I thank him and take a sip. I swallow and cough, my eyes watering. "Oh wow," I croak. "That's strong."

"She told me to use the good stuff and double it. That'll be eighteen dollars."

I cough again, and rifle through my purse for cash. "That's a little rich considering the atmosphere." I pull a twenty out of my wallet and put it on the counter. "Wait, who told you to use the good stuff?"

The bartender turns and points to the end of the bar that had the abandoned beer bottle five minutes ago. Toni is there, and she raises her beer bottle to me. A flurry of butterflies take flight in my stomach. She slides off her stool and strolls over.

"Hi." She leans against the bar, all relaxed charm.

My hello comes out breathy and my blush feels like the heat of a thousand suns on my face and neck.

Toni pushes the twenty back to me. "I've never seen you here before. New to town?" She drinks from her beer bottle, eyes on mine.

So, we're doing this.

"No, here for business."

"What do you do?"

"Import/export."

She looks me up and down with a wry smile. "You don't look like a mobster, so that must mean you're with the CIA."

I lean forward and whisper. "I'll never tell." I very quietly, subtly, inhale, hoping to catch a whiff of the scent that hides in the hollow behind Toni's ear. It's faint but enough to activate a stirring deep inside me. I pull back. "What do you do?"

She's smirking, and I know I've been busted, but don't give a damn. I stare right into her eyes and dare her to go all in. The change in her demeanor is slight. When her tongue licks her bottom lip, I know exactly where this will end.

"I'm the vice president of Fourteener Sports."

Her answer oozes confidence, and my heart swells with pride for Toni. No matter what happens in the future between us, that week we worked together, what we accomplished, set her on this new path. We were a great team.

"Impressive," I say. I swallow down the emotions that clog my throat.

"I had a good mentor," she replies.

"Good mentors are hard to find."

Toni's eyes search my face, linger on my lips. "Yes, they are." Her eyes find mine and there's a tiny spark I haven't seen lately. "I don't know your name."

Do it, Audrey. Go all in.

"Roxanne."

Toni grins. She's surprised and loves it. "Roxanne? I hope you aren't the Roxanne that picked up my best friend on Saturday night."

I laugh. "No, I'm not."

"It's not a common name. Are you sure?"

"Positive."

"Hmm." Toni looks me up and down openly now that the game is on. "Too bad. My friend has been walking around in a daze for the last couple of days. I'm Max."

"Max."

I take my time surveying Toni from head to toe, seeing beneath the hiking pants and flannel to the smooth hard body beneath. I linger on her breasts, my heart racing, my tongue desperate to feel her hardened nipple scrape against it. When our eyes finally meet, her pupils are blown with desire, the electric blue of her irises smaller than I've ever seen them. I raise an eyebrow. Time to slow it down a bit.

"Is that short for anything?"

Her voice is strangled when she answers. "I'm sorry?"

"Max. What is it short for?"

"Oh, nothing. A childhood nickname." Toni moves closer and rests her arm on the back of my barstool. "I have an early flight tomorrow."

"Oh?"

"I was going to grab something to eat." She pauses, her gaze going to my lips. "Then go to bed."

"Early night, huh?"

"Yes. Are you hungry, Roxanne?"

"Starving. Do you know somewhere nearby I can get something to eat?"

Toni's voice is low. "My place is around the corner."

"Are you a good cook?"

"I am." She's so close I can see tiny orange flecks in her eyes that I've never seen before. "I'm especially good at making sure my guests are fully satisfied by the time they leave."

I bite the corner of my lower lip and Toni's breath catches.

"With an offer like that, how can I refuse?"

"Audrey?"

"Hmm?"

"I have to leave. I have a plane to catch."

I'm on my stomach; a warm hand gently strokes my bare back. I open my eyes and see Toni looking down at me, a strange expression on her face. It wakes me up a little. I didn't realize I'd fallen asleep.

"What?"

"I have to go."

Right. Toni has a plane to catch. "Oh." I try to sit up, but I think my bones have dissolved. "I need to go, too."

"No, no. It's before five. Go back to sleep. Lock the door-knob behind you when you leave. I'll have Max come over and lock the deadbolt later."

"Oh, OK."

My God I'm so tired I can hardly think; I barely understand what Toni is saying.

"I'll be gone a couple of weeks," Toni says. "Um, maybe we can talk when I get back. Or you can call me if you want to. Or... or not." She pauses, opens her mouth, closes it. She smiles, but it doesn't reach her eyes. "This was... fun. Bye."

She pats me on the shoulder, and is gone.

CHAPTER THIRTY

AUDREY

It's barely past six when I walk into the house and run into Willa walking out, dressed and ready for work.

"Well, she made it home finally," Willa says, grinning. "I guess it went—" Her expression falls. "Audrey, what happened?"

"She said it was fun, and left." I burst into the tears I'd been holding in on the drive over.

Willa drops her computer bag and takes me into her arms. "Oh, sweetie."

She ushers me into the kitchen, sits me down at the table, and makes me a cup of coffee. When she's seated next to me, I tell her what happened. Every little detail. Probably more than she wants to know, to be honest. By the time I'm done, my grief at the comment has changed a bit to anger.

"How could she do that? Tell me it was 'fun' and then leave. It was raw and emotional and when she looked at me, Willa, she didn't have to say a word. I just ca—"

Willa holds up a hand. "OK, OK. I really don't need the details again."

"It wasn't just sex. We made love. It was life-changing.

Jesus, I literally couldn't walk. She had to carry me into the bedroom."

"Well, that's hot."

"Right? It was like I weighed nothing. She just scooped me up and carried me to her bed. If I wasn't totally in love with her before I would have been right then."

"Did you tell her that?"

"What?"

"That you love her?"

"Well, no. I could barely think. After she, you know, I fell asleep."

"So, let me see if I have this straight. Toni suggested role-playing the first night you were together. Said it would be fun."

"Yes."

"She mentioned it again, obliquely, yesterday, said it could be fun. You went to the Chicken Head to see if she was sending you a signal."

"Yes."

"You two role-played, picked each other up, had amazing sex, you fell asleep."

"Yes."

"Instead of just leaving without saying goodbye, Toni wakes you up, tells you she had fun, and leaves."

"Right."

"Why would Toni think you wanted anything but fun? She made it pretty clear yesterday when she said 'It could be fun' that she wasn't looking for or expecting anything more."

"Because that was not 'role-playing and picking someone up at a bar' sex. It meant something."

Willa looks me in the eye for a long moment. "Maybe it didn't to her," she says quietly.

I gasp. How could she say something so awful to me right now? That wasn't what I wanted to hear, that it meant nothing to Toni. That the love in her eyes when she looked up at me was fake, her tenderness when she carried me into the bedroom was part of a ruse, or that the way she caressed my back as I fell asleep in her arms... you didn't do any of those things with a woman you were just "having fun" with.

My breath catches in my throat. Maybe this is what Toni does. She's had fun, no-strings-attached sex with dozens of women over the years, many of whom have had a hard time letting go. Maybe she looks at every woman the way she looked at me.

"She's probably protecting her heart, Audrey," Willa says. "Can you blame her? It's only been two months since Christmas. The last time she opened up, and I'm using your words here, you put a stake through her heart. Toni isn't about to put her heart on the line again. Been there, done that, got the participation trophy. It's your turn to put your heart on the line."

"That's what I did, meeting her at the bar."

"No, you role-played as different people and picked her up. Did you tell her you loved her?"

"I didn't have time."

"You could have told her instead of role-playing," Willa says. "Why didn't you?"

I open my mouth to respond, but have nothing to say. No answer whatsoever.

"Yep. That's what I thought." Willa stands and puts her computer backpack over her shoulder.

"Where are you going?" I ask.

"Work."

"It's barely six thirty in the morning."

"I'm trying to beat Greta into the office."

"Why?" I ask.

Willa gives me a Cheshire Cat grin. "Because it will piss her off." She walks down the hall toward the garage.

"Would you two just fuck and get it over with?" I ask, more than a little irritated that Willa is leaving me.

"This is much more fun," she says over her shoulder.

She's closing the door behind her when I call out, "Says the woman who has been celibate for five years!"

The door is almost closed, but opens up a bit. Willa sticks her arm through the door, gives me the bird, then closes it behind her. A second later she opens it back up and sticks her head through. "You know what you need to do, Audrey."

"No, I don't!"

"When you figure it out, you know where to find me."

With that, Willa is gone. I hear the garage door rise and close.

I put my head down on the kitchen table. She's right. I should have just told Toni I love her the moment I saw her. I expected to have time later. How would I have known I was going to fall asleep so quickly? I assumed we would have time to talk like we did the first night. I smile, remembering the intimacy we shared after making love the first time. Our hands lightly touching, talking quietly, joking, smiling. My smile widens at her description of fair ups, and I laugh. So competitive, even when it comes to orgasms. I lift my head. What is our orgasm tally? I'm pretty sure she's ahead.

Well, that won't do at all.

It's time I even the score, in more ways than one.

Twenty minutes later, wearing the same clothes I wore to work the day before, I walk into Greta's office. Willa is there, sitting at her computer at the small conference table, Greta looking over her shoulder at the computer screen. They look up in surprise when I walk in.

"Greta, I need some hiking boots."

CHAPTER THIRTY-ONE

TONI

For the first time in my life, the last place I want to be is on a mountain.

I had fun.

I cringe every time I think about those words coming out of my mouth. As if making love to Audrey could ever be described as merely "fun." Life-changing, world-shaking, heartbreaking... all of those words describe being with her two nights ago. A colossal mistake is also a good description. Much nicer than Max's *You are such a fucking idiot* comment.

I called Max from the airport at six a.m., which might explain her less than supportive response. "I didn't think she'd show," I said.

"How big of a part of you was hoping she would show up and confess her undying love?"

"Just a little," I mumbled.

"Liar," Max said, but her voice was kind. "I know you are in love, or think you are, but she's using you, Toni, and you're letting her."

"Maybe *I'm* using *her*," I said.

"Sure, because that sounds *just* like you."

"It's not like Audrey, either."

"Hmm. You didn't tell her you loved her during this magical night of sex, did you?"

"No, I'm not that stupid. I left before she was out of bed. I told her I had fun, and left."

"I'm proud of you."

"I'm not. It was awful."

"No, meaningless sex is exactly what Audrey wants, and you know it."

"It was not meaningless, and you are *not* helping."

"If by 'not helping' you mean I'm not feeding into your delusions of one true love and grand gestures of reconciliation, then you're absolutely right. I'm not helping."

"I cannot wait until you fall in love and get your heart broken." I grimaced. "OK, that came out really bad."

Max laughed. "I know what you mean; when it happens you're going to be a cold-hearted bitch, just like me. I own it. But I'm not going to be stupid enough to fall in love."

"Famous last words, Max. Tell me what to do."

"Nothing. The ball has been in her court since Christmas. Still is." I heard Max shift around in her bed. When she spoke again her voice was a little muffled. "I think you should go to New Zealand, find a pretty woman who will be more than willing to take your mind off your heartbreak for a night or two."

I gave some sort of non-committal grunt and told her my plane was boarding.

I purchased Wi-Fi on every leg of the journey, keeping my phone on and available for texts, hoping that maybe, just maybe, Audrey would text me.

She didn't. Of course she didn't. But like an idiot, I kept checking anyway, my heart breaking each time there wasn't a new message.

Now, it's twenty-eight hours of travel later and I'm waiting in the lobby of the hotel with the local tour operator to meet the trekkers who signed up for a ten-day inn-to-inn hiking tour of the west coast of New Zealand.

"Everyone's here, right?" I ask Kaia Thomason, the owner of the company I am here to evaluate as a potential partner for Fourteener Trekking.

"We're missing one. The woman who signed up yesterday."

"I thought ten hikers was the limit. Do you make exceptions a lot?" I ask. All the potential safety issues that can arise from having too many people on a hike scroll through my mind, and I mentally put a tick in the con list of my evaluation.

"Never," Kaia says.

"Then why—"

"I'm here, I'm here! Don't leave!"

My head jerks around and there's Audrey, red-faced and out of breath, loaded down with enough camping and hiking gear to last two weeks on a through hike. She's dressed head to toe in clothes from Fourteener's upcoming fall line by the looks of it, and her hiking boots are so new the soles squeak when she walks. She has a multicolored bandanna tied around her long neck. Her backpack is top of the line, and is absolutely stuffed with God knows what because she has practically another backpack's worth of gear hanging off of every possible hook on the outside of the pack.

She looks absolutely ridiculous, and she's never looked more beautiful.

Everyone is stunned into silence by her appearance, including me. She looks around the group, in a bit of a panic, until her eyes find mine. I'm standing in the back of the room, trying like hell to slow my hammering heart. I don't think she came all this way to chew me out about leaving her in my bed naked and wrecked and gorgeous with *It was fun!* but I also wouldn't be surprised if she did. She smiles and her body sags in relief. For a second, I'm afraid that her gear is going to topple her over. I'm not entirely sure how she got it all on in the first place.

"Here, let me help you." A man named George hops up and helps Audrey out of her pack and sets it against the wall next to her.

Audrey thanks him, rolls her shoulders a bit, and smiles.

One of the young women in the group who's been on her phone the entire time raises her hand like we're in school, and says, "Um, I, like thought that all the gear was included in the price?"

"It is," Kaia says. "There must have been some miscommunication somewhere along the way."

Audrey looks confused for a moment, gazing around at her fellow hikers, all of whom are dressed for the welcome dinner we are about to have at a local Māori restaurant, and not for hiking. She must see the grin I'm trying to hold back because I know exactly where the miscommunication came from. My sister.

Audrey grins and shakes her head. "Greta wanted to make sure I was prepared for every situation."

"I can see that," I say.

"As far as pranks go, it's pretty epic. I didn't know Greta had it in her." Audrey's expression turns hesitant, unsure. "Hi," she says.

"Hi." I feel like a teenager talking to a girl I'm crushing on at the school dance. "What are you doing here, Audrey? You hate hiking."

A couple of people in the group gasp, and Audrey chuckles. She looks at them. "It's true. I hate hiking." She turns her gaze on me and our eyes lock. Everyone else in the room disappears. "But I love you, Toni Danzig, and I couldn't let another day go by without telling you."

My throat is clogged with emotion. I can't speak; I can barely think. I can still hear, though, and after everyone has gasped in surprise, one of the young women in the group says in a stage whisper, "Oh my God, it's a grand gesture."

"What's a grand gesture?" George asks loudly.

Everyone cracks up, but no one as loudly as Audrey and me. My laughter is nerves, giddiness, hope, all wrapped together.

"Shh, it's a romance novel thing."

"Like *Outlander*," George says again. "You love *Outlander*, Gwen."

"Shh, George, you're ruining it," someone—probably Gwen—says.

Audrey and I are laughing, but we haven't moved, or taken our eyes off each other. There are two couches, a coffee table, a chair, and ten very invested onlookers between us. I shrug slightly and raise my eyebrows.

Audrey shakes her head and laughs. "In for a penny, in for a pound."

"Oh, this is *so* going on TikTok," the young woman says.

"No, it's not," Kaia says. "Let's head to the restaurant."

There's some mild grumbling and good-natured jokes about missing the best part of the Hallmark movie, but Kaia manages to herd them all out of the lobby. "You know where we're going, yeah?" she asks me.

I nod and tell her I'll see her there soon.

Finally, Audrey and I are alone.

Audrey closes her eyes, inhales, and exhales. When her eyes open again, there's a hint of sadness in them. "I am so sorry I hurt you. I wish I could say I didn't mean to, but I did. It was the only way I knew to protect myself, to push you away so you wouldn't come back. I'd learned my lesson about not being clear enough, or not being listened to, and didn't want to make that mistake again.

"But then you didn't come back, and I wasn't prepared for the huge gaping hole you left in my life. In my heart. You weren't there physically, but everywhere I turned something reminded me of you, or someone was talking about you, telling a story, or missing you at the office. No one missed you as much as I did. I missed seeing you sitting on the edge of someone's desk, giving them your undivided attention, making them laugh, putting a smile on their face. I missed the way you tease Greta and she pretends to get irritated about it. I missed catching you looking at me with those gorgeous eyes of yours, grinning, and sticking your tongue out at me so maybe I wouldn't see what you were feeling. You are the sweetest, kindest, most selfless woman I've ever known and I think I fell in love with you the first night we were together but I was too messed up and too scared and too belligerent to see it. To open up my heart to you. These last two months have shown me what my life is like without you and I hate it. There's no joy, no passion, no fun, no laughter. So, I flew eight thousand miles, with two thousand dollars' worth of useless gear, to tell you how much I love you, ask your forgiveness, and hope you'll give me another chance. And to go hiking with you."

Audrey has inched her way across the room and stands close enough to me that I can see the smudges of mascara under her eyes. I could pull her into my arms if I wanted to.

I'm searching her face, taking her all in, seeing our future together spool out in front of us. I'm enjoying my fantasy of long walks, and snuggling on the couch, and cooking dinners together, but to Audrey, I'm merely silent.

She swallows. "Toni? Say something. Please."

I pull her into my arms. Audrey releases a little "oh" of surprise, then settles against me. A perfect fit. She wraps her arms around my neck and grins mischievously.

I cup her jaw and say, "You had me at *I'm here.*"

A LETTER FROM LAURA

Dear reader,

I want to say a huge thank you for choosing to read *About Last Night*. If you did enjoy it, and want to keep up to date with all my latest releases, just sign up at the following link. Your email address will never be shared and you can unsubscribe at any time.

www.bookouture.com/laura-henry

I hope you loved *About Last Night* and if you did I would be very grateful if you could write a review, on as many sites as possible (Amazon, Goodreads, Google Play, Apple Books, etc). Reviews are for readers, not authors, and they make an enormous difference helping new readers to discover one of my books for the first time.

I would love to hear directly from you, too! There is nothing better than waking up to an email or social media message about my books from a reader! The best way to contact me is through my website; that way your message will come straight to my inbox. Or you can contact me through Facebook or Instagram. I look forward to hearing from you!

Happy reading!

Laura Henry

KEEP IN TOUCH WITH LAURA

www.melissalenhardt.net

 facebook.com/ReadLauraHenry

instagram.com/readlaurahenry

ACKNOWLEDGMENTS

First to my friends and family for supporting me through a rather tumultuous 2023. When life brings you lemons, have a squad of people who know how to make lemonade, and that one friend who will sneakily spike it.

Specifically, I'd like to thank my US agent, Alice Speilburg, and my UK agent, Anna Carmichael. Thanks to Allison Carroll at Audible for helping bring Audrey and Toni's story to life the first time in audio, and to Maisie Lawrence for helping me expand their story and give it a second life in print! To the team at Bookouture who have been incredibly supportive and enthusiastic about bringing Audrey and Toni's romance to the UK market, and the world!

Finally, to my readers. I hope you enjoyed Toni and Audrey's story! They'll be back, in a smaller role, for the sequel, which tells Willa and Greta's story. Yes, you will find out what happened between them on Christmas Eve very soon. Stay tuned, and thank you for reading!

PUBLISHING TEAM

Turning a manuscript into a book requires the efforts of many people. The publishing team at Bookouture would like to acknowledge everyone who contributed to this publication.

Commercial
Lauren Morrissette
Hannah Richmond
Imogen Allport

Cover design
Rachel Lawston

Data and analysis
Mark Alder
Mohamed Bussuri

Editorial
Maisie Lawrence
Ria Clare

Copyeditor
Anne O'Brien

Proofreader
Becca Allen

Printed in Great Britain
by Amazon